"Brittany, there's a glow about you," Sam said, catching her hand and drawing her down beside him.

"That's dust, Sam."

"Then it's fairy dust, because it's doing strange things to me."

"Do you have to sneeze?" she asked teasingly, aware of the slow heat building between them.

He leaned forward so he could look directly into her face. Her green eyes were shining and the soft tangle of her hair framed her flushed cheeks. He curled one hand around her neck and held her gently. "Oh, Brittany, you are without a doubt the most beautiful creature I've ever known." His breath caught in his throat, and for a second Sam Lawrence felt an astonishing sensation: the stinging wonder of tears at the power Brittany had to move him.

Searching his deep eyes, Brittany watched the play of his emotions. His eyes almost seemed to change color, then deepen in intensity until she felt mesmerized. "Sam."

His fingers delved into her silky hair and he bit back a groan. Desire flared deep within him and he fought for control. "What, Brittany?"

"Are you . . . habit-forming?"

He smiled. "Let me show you. . . ."

WHAT ARE *LOVESWEPT* ROMANCES?

They are stories of true romance and touching emotion. We believe those two very important ingredients are constants in our highly sensual and very believable stories in the *LOVESWEPT* line. Our goal is to give you, the reader, stories of consistently high quality that may sometimes make you laugh, sometimes make you cry, but are always fresh and creative and contain many delightful surprises within their pages.

Most romance fans read an enormous number of books. Those they truly love, they keep. Others may be traded with friends and soon forgotten. We hope that each *LOVESWEPT* romance will be a treasure—a "keeper." We will always try to publish

LOVE STORIES YOU'LL NEVER FORGET
BY AUTHORS YOU'LL ALWAYS REMEMBER

The Editors

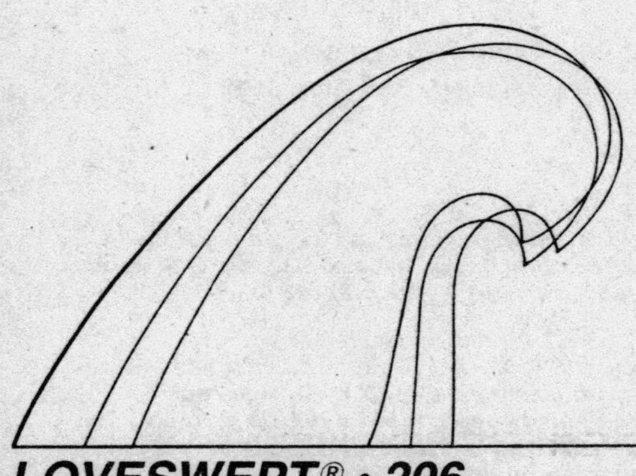

LOVESWEPT® • 206

Sally Goldenbaum

A Dream to Cling To

BANTAM BOOKS
TORONTO • NEW YORK • LONDON • SYDNEY • AUCKLAND

A DREAM TO CLING TO
A Bantam Book / September 1987

If you would be interested in receiving protective vinyl covers for your Loveswept books, please write to this address for information:

Loveswept
Bantam Books
P.O. Box 985
Hicksville, NY 11802

ISBN 0-553-21841-7

Published simultaneously in the United States and Canada

Bantam Books are published by Bantam Books, Inc. Its trademark, consisting of the words "Bantam Books" and the portrayal of a rooster, is Registered in U.S. Patent and Trademark Office and in other countries. Marca Registrada. Bantam Books, Inc., 666 Fifth Avenue, New York, New York 10103.

PRINTED IN THE UNITED STATES OF AMERICA

O 0 9 8 7 6 5 4 3 2 1

One

Sam Lawrence pulled his lanky frame out of the Queen Anne chair and walked over to the fireplace. The leaping flames felt good against his legs and eased his cramped joints, stiff from sitting too long in the Winters' ornately carved chairs. He thought of the neglected stack of work piled up in his office and the pressured rush of getting the Winters job done on time. Things would be tight for a while. He stared down at the scuffed toes of his boots. There'd be no time to get away and really loosen the joints, free the mind. Sam wasn't accustomed to the cramped feeling that was heavy on his spirit. Oh, well, there'd always be later. Slowly he raised his head and smiled.

"Well," he said, his gaze moving from one member of the family to another, "what do you say we call it a night? We'll need to get together a few times to gather those anecdotes and stories that'll give the game its life. And in addition to interviewing family and friends, I'll need one of you to work closely with me to make sure I'm on the right track as we move along." Even when he was at his most serious, like now, Sam's deep voice held a hint of laughter. He smiled encouragingly. "The information will come.

Sometimes it takes a little time to prime the pump, you know."

"Prime the pump?" Katherine Winters echoed, her silvery voice curling upward.

"Oh, but don't worry, Mrs. Winters, it'll come. It always does." He flashed the older woman an engaging grin, then shoved his hands deep into the pockets of his corduroy pants and leaned back against the carved mahogany mantel. Sure it did, he thought. Anyone who had risen to the business heights of a Gordon Winters had color in his life . . . didn't he? Sam rubbed the rough stubble of a beard that seemed to have appeared since his arrival at the lavish, lovely Winters home well over an hour ago.

"Surely, *surely* Brittany Ellsbeth will be here soon," Mrs. Winters said. She lifted her thin brows hopefully and gazed around at the others, seeking assurance that this was in fact the case.

Sam noticed that no one seemed willing to chance confirmation of the eldest Winters child's arrival.

"Brittany always has plenty of stories to tell," Mrs. Winters added brightly. "You see, she's a lot like her father. She'll understand what you need in order to make the game about Gordon. You'll see, Mr. Lawrence. Just as soon as she gets here . . ."

"If she doesn't make it, Mother, she'll make it next time." Sara Winters Hancock smiled comfortingly at her mother. "You know Brittany. She tends to get involved in things and sometimes forgets."

Mrs. Winters sat still, her thin, frail hands knotted together in her lap as she returned her newly married daughter's smile. "Yes . . . yes, Sara, she does, doesn't she?" She looked over at Sam. "It's all those animals, you see. . . . Perhaps if we give her just a few more minutes."

"Well." He shifted his weight from one leg to the other and glanced down at his empty notepad. He rotated one shoulder beneath his heavy sweater and tried to ease away the tiredness. Then he grinned at Katherine Winters and shrugged. "Well, okay, sure, Mrs. Winters. If you're not too tired, we'll give it a little longer. Maybe we can get some more thoughts down while we wait."

"Yes, I'm sure we can!" Mrs. Winters assured him, and Sam could see how relieved she was that he was willing to wait for the errant daughter, now nearly an hour late. Sam usually wasn't big on punching time clocks himself. Except at night, when he had trouble keeping his eyes open much after nine. Like now. He stifled a yawn behind one hand and stretched out his legs. Then he settled back to business.

His thick brows drew into a line above his eyes as he looked from Sara to her husband, Michael, who was the perfect solicitous bridegroom, never moving far from Sara's side. Their hands kept finding each other across the sofa pillows and Sam knew they were just as eager as he to get home. Probably more so, he decided with a lopsided smile. They were a nice bunch, these Winters folks. He hadn't known quite what to expect when the game job for Gordon Winters had come his way. Most of the games he'd done about people had been on a much smaller scale. Hell, half had been favors to friends and he'd never charged for them! But this one could be important.

He'd tried to learn a little about the family from the society pages, but after a quick look he'd trashed the papers and the idea. Not fair. No one was as flat as a columnist's type. And he was right. These were good people, not flat at all. Now, if only he could figure out how to shake up their imaginations . . .

"Okay, folks, everybody ready?"

"Sure. Shoot, Sam." Gordon Junior stretched his arms above his head. "Throw some more questions our way. We'll come up with something." He grinned encouragingly.

Sam nodded a thanks and looked down at his pad as

he rubbed the kinks out of the back of his neck. "Let's go back to hobbies."

He glanced around the room and drew his audience into his deepening gaze as the tiredness was suspended and the showman in Sam took over. "Hobbies are a great source of stories—they tell a lot about a man! Now, think everyone, what does Mr. Winters do in his spare time?"

"Doze."

"Work."

"Fish."

Sam dove desperately onto the last comment and spoke in exclamations to keep the spark alive. "Fish! All right, folks, now we're cookin'! Fish stories are great! And every fisherman has some of those wild tales that curl your hair and raise your eyebrows." He pushed a handful of thick sandy hair off his forehead and smiled with anticipation.

Sara crossed her legs with great care and looked over at her brother. "Gordie, I think you know more about this area than I. I've never . . . well, I never much liked fishing. . . ."

Gordie twined his fingers together beneath his chin in deep thought. "Sure, sure. Well, let's see. It rained one year, I think, and he came back early." He looked over at his mother.

Katherine Winters sighed, her tiny brows pulling together and wrinkling the still-beautiful pale skin of her forehead. She raised her head to look at Sam. "He . . . he fishes with Brittany."

The hope fizzled out of Sam. "Oh." He should have known. Sure, he fished with Brittany, like he *rode* with Brittany, and explored old maritime museums with Brittany. And that was, unfortunately, the sum total of what Sam Lawrence knew thus far about the Winters scion. How the hell was he supposed to design a board game around the life of a man whose family's most exciting memory was that he didn't fish in the rain?

Sam looked around the room for the twentieth time that night and swallowed the rest of his drink in a single gulp. Raking one hand through his hair, he straightened his stance before the fire. "Well, folks, where the Sam Hill *is* Brittany?"

Katherine Winters looked up so suddenly at the unexpected words that her sherry sloshed over the edge of the fine Waterford crystal and darkened her silk dress. "Oh, dear," she murmured.

Sam smiled apologetically. "Sorry, everyone. It's been a long day."

"Don't worry about it, Mr. Lawrence," Sara said. "The problem is that Brittany sometimes gets deterred, you see, waylaid by some other pressing concern. But she always shows up, sooner or la—"

A gust of wind and the slamming of the huge door in the front hallway halted Sara's prophetic words midstream.

Brittany Ellsbeth Winters swept into the room, her cheeks pinked from the cold, her green eyes sparkling brightly. "Hi, everyone. I'm terribly sorry to be late!" She dropped her bag by the door, then bent over and hugged her mother warmly.

"Brittany dear, I was beginning to worry about you."

Brittany brushed the back of one hand along her mother's pale cheek and scolded her affectionately. "You know better than to worry about me, Mother! I know your message said 'urgent,' but things never seem to go according to schedule these days. It was Jerry Fitzgerald's eighty-fifth birthday—can you believe that?—and he's as sharp as you or I. He wanted me to bring some of the animals out to the Elms Senior Citizens Home for the birthday party, so—"

Brittany's words halted abruptly as she lifted her head to smile at the rest of the family. Instead, her glance fell soundly into the amused gaze of a tall, lanky stranger, his arm draped casually on the mantel. His lazy smile seemed to warm the air between them.

She straightened up slowly. "Oh. Hello. I'm sorry, I didn't see you standing there." A slight, embarrassed smile tipped the edges of her mouth. Who was this person? She glanced at the shadow of his beard covering a strong, square chin, and smiled to herself. He looked so . . . well, strong and *unregistered.* And his hair curled over the edge of his sweater. Mother must think him a hippie! She held out her hand and took a step toward the stranger.

"I didn't realize we had a guest. I'm Brittany Winters."

"The prodigal daughter," Sam murmured, then strode forward to take the slender hand between his. He'd been right about one thing: Gordon Winters's life *did* have color to it. But he'd been damn wrong about how he'd imagined Brittany Winters up to this moment. He knew from the brief family bio that she was the first born—late twenties, if he remembered correctly, although she seemed younger. And the woman lighting the room around him wasn't any silver-spooned society girl, as he'd expected. He inhaled her clean, enticing scent and felt the tight cramp in his shoulders begin to disappear. No, this was no pampered girl, not with that shy smile that breathed of blue skies and wildflowers. He swallowed hard. She was a woodland creature, so soft-looking, with a tangle of thick curls in shades of dark spun gold and auburn. She was lovely. "I am happy to meet you, Brittany Winters."

"Do I know you?" Brittany's smile wavered as she found herself concentrating intently on the warm cave his hands made around her own. Tilting her head back, she gazed searchingly at his rugged features. Silly question, she thought. This face she wouldn't easily forget. "You are . . . ?"

"Sam Lawrence."

"Oh." Her gaze continued to explore the face that didn't fit here in this elegantly decorated house. She spoke slowly around the tightness in her throat. "Well, hello, Mr. Lawrence." Quickly she slipped her hand from between his and curled it into a fist. The roughness of his fingers lingered, warm and tingly on her skin.

"Brittany," Sara's light voice intruded, "Mr. Lawrence is here to help with the company's retirement gift for Father."

"Retirement gift . . ." Brittany repeated, still unsure of Sam's presence. She looked quickly around the room. "Where is Dad?"

Mrs. Winters leaned forward in her chair. "He's in Boston, darling, settling a dispute in the plant there. That's why we chose tonight to meet with Mr. Lawrence. He's come up with a *wonderful* present for Gordon."

"Oh, I see," Brittany said, but she didn't really see at all. What kind of gift could a Sam Lawrence possibly help with? "Well, that's good. Heaven knows, Dad deserves a great gift." When she looked back at Sam, she noticed his eyes, so brown and clear and bottomless, they seemed to look right inside of her. She shivered and rubbed her palms down the soft folds of her skirt. "Do you work for my father?"

"Oh, no, dear," Mrs. Winters answered quickly. "Mr. Lawrence has been hired by the firm's board to execute the gift." She smiled gently, then shook her white head and looked up at Sam. "Mr. Lawrence, you explain it so much better."

Sam nodded kindly at the gentle lady who was the reason he hadn't walked out of the mansion a long time ago. Then he turned his close attention to the reason he was willing to stay on—indefinitely. "Ms. Winters—"

"Brittany, please," she interrupted with a throaty laugh. Brittany slipped down into a chair near the fire and welcomed the firm support beneath her. When she looked up, her gaze passed over Sam, from his well-worn boots to his face. She knew she'd never seen him before in her entire life, yet there was a strange feeling of connection, of association, that unsettled her. What was it? And *who* was he? Sam Lawrence looked like he'd be good at "executing" a hike up Mt. Washington, but a retirement gift? "Please go on, Mr. Lawrence," she urged.

"Sure thing." Sam nodded, then shoved his hands back into his pockets and watched the firelight dance off Brittany's gold-flecked eyes. Or did the fire begin there . . . ?

"Well," he began slowly, his gaze never leaving her face, "as I told the others, this won't be your ordinary plaque or gold watch or around-the-world-vacation type of retirement gift."

"Good, Dad isn't ordinary." Brittany smiled, but she was puzzled. It was a sales pitch, not what she would have expected from the uneven-featured man with the shadow of a beard and the mischievous sparkle in his eyes.

Sam noticed the hint of formality that had crept into her voice and continued, suddenly enjoying the silent game they were playing with each other, the unspoken assumptions, the subtle evaluations. As he rubbed his chin thoughtfully, still gazing directly at her, he slid down onto the gold brocade love seat opposite her chair. He leaned forward, his arms resting on his knees, which nearly brushed her own.

"What my company is putting together for your father, Brittany, is a tailor-made, personal board game of his life."

Surprised, Brittany sat up, her back reed-straight and her face expressionless. "A game?"

Sam nodded. She was watching him so attentively, it nearly fogged his thoughts. "A game about Mr. Winters, using his life—your family's life—as content. You know, kind of a *This Is Your Life* in game form." He'd given that explanation dozens, maybe hundreds of times, and this was when his listeners usually jumped in and told him what a terrific idea it was and my, oh, my, wasn't he a creative son of a gun!

Brittany Winters was silent.

Sam smiled, and a dimple flashed in his cheek. Well, now, this just might be the challenge he needed to get the juices flowing! "Do you get the hang of it, Brittany?" He watched her carefully and fought back the urge to move closer, to slip his fingers into the soft mass of hair that framed her face and relieve her of the sudden tenseness that now lined her full mouth.

"A game about my father's life?" Brittany asked softly, her gaze leaving his face, shifting down to ponder the herringbone pattern in her skirt. She studied the angled lines intently, rubbing along them with one finger, then slowly raised her head and looked questioningly at her mother.

"Isn't it a lovely idea, dear? The board has already appropriated the money and now it's up to Mr. Lawrence here to collect the information. It's a fine present." Katherine Winters smiled firmly. "Now, Brittany, will you tell us what you think?"

Brittany looked from her mother to Sam. She nibbled thoughtfully on her bottom lip. "A game, you say?"

Her voice was low but sharper now, Sam noticed, and the shyness in her eyes had disappeared.

"Yes. What *do* you think of the idea, Brittany?"

His voice was deep and unnervingly intimate. She stood and stared into the fire for a moment, then turned slowly back to him. "It's a quaint idea, Mr. Lawrence, and I don't mean any offense, but I'm not sure it's the appropriate gift for my father's retirement. He likes horses, fishing, books—things like that." She smiled faintly, then looked apologetically at her mother.

She knew Sam was watching her carefully. He cocked his head and pulled his long, loose-limbed body up from the delicate love seat; his dark eyes lit with curiosity and a hint of laughter. "So, Brittany, you don't like the idea?"

"Like it?" The words tumbled out too quickly. No, she didn't like it especially. And she knew it was an instinctive reaction that wasn't the least bit objective. What people had done in their lives was a private matter—at least she'd kept her own life that way. And making a game out of someone's life simply didn't sit right. It was a unique idea, she admitted, but uncomfortable. Besides, she rationalized, her father didn't even play poker. What would he do with a board game? No, it wasn't just that, she told herself. Face it. It was this Sam Lawrence, a brown-eyed stranger sifting through her life. That was what was disturbing her. "No," she said more firmly. "I don't like the idea."

Sam bit back a grin. This soft lovely creature had spunk as well as the magic of a goddess. And the longer she stood there like that with her eyes glinting gold from the firelight and her cheeks flushed, the higher went the stakes. It wasn't just the job now—it was moving through just a bit of life's winding stream with Brittany Winters beside him that he didn't want to give up. His eyes lingered on her face while he rubbed his jaw thoughtfully. "I see. Well, maybe if you'd give me a little time, Brittany, I could explain it better."

Brittany forced a gracious smile and shook her head. "I'm sorry, but that's my opinion."

"But not the board of director's, dear," her mother said softly. "They want this, and we shall all help it come about."

Brittany took a deep breath and shrugged her shoulders. She could see the matter was settled, and probably had been long before she arrived. "All right." The silent vow she took to stay as far away from this family project as she could was hidden behind the quick sweep of her lashes as she lowered her head. Why was she fighting this so? she wondered. And why did Sam's nearness disturb her? Things were usually so clear to her: her goals, her life, her likes and dislikes. But tonight she had walked directly into a thick fog, and the feeling was strangely disturbing.

"Hey, Britt, I think it'll be fun," her brother said. "Here, have a drink."

She shook her head. "No, thank you, Gordie. I have to leave now." She edged her way toward the door, avoiding Sam Lawrence's eyes. "Let me know if you want me to fill out a questionnaire or something."

"There's one more thing, Brittany dear."

She looked back at her mother cautiously. There was a strange tone to Katherine Winters's voice, and it made Brittany slightly uneasy. "Yes, Mother?"

"Mr. Lawrence needs one of us to work very closely with him in order to make sense out of everything. To be a 'right-hand man' as his brochure explained it." Katherine Winters smiled.

Brittany choked. It was the same smile her mother had used years ago when she'd announced unexpectedly that arrangements had been made for Brittany to make her society debut. That had been one of the lowest moments of Brittany's life, but she had a queasy suspicion it was about to move into second place. Oh, if only she'd stayed on for Mr. Fitzgerald's birthday cake.

"And since you have such a flexible schedule," her mother continued, "we've all agreed you're the perfect choice to help Mr. Lawrence create this wonderful game."

Brittany spun around and looked at Gordie and Sara. They smiled. Then she turned to the man who was stepping into her life.

He was leaning nonchalantly against the mantel, one elbow resting on its polished surface. His face was expressionless, except one brow lifted questioningly. "What do you say, Brittany?"

She bit down so forcibly on her lip that she nearly

jumped. She looked back at her mother, whose serene smile was still in place. She elected to answer her mother instead.

"Mother, I can't. I have my job." But she knew as soon as she spoke that no one was listening. Taking pets to old folks' homes for visits—even if she was being paid for it!—wasn't a job, not really. Getting married and planning for babies like Sara did, that was a job. Or studying for the bar exam, like Gordie was doing.

Sam was at her side now, his hand resting casually on her shoulder. A small intense circle of heat melted into her.

"Hey, Brittany, I understand. This was all kind of thrown on you. But I really do need your help. Honest. And I'll try hard not to impose on your time."

His eyes were so incredibly deep that for a moment Brittany couldn't concentrate on what he was saying. When she finally spoke, her voice was soft and deliberate. "Oh, but you don't quite understand, Mr. Lawrence. I don't *have* any time to impose upon. My days are filled, you see." She clasped her hands behind her back and feigned a calmness she hadn't felt since entering the house. Would it be awful to shake his hand off of her shoulder so she could think clearly? She wet her bottom lip. "And I'm really not a very good person to work on a game. I play tennis, but not board games." She laughed, and it sounded thin to her. "I never even played bridge in college."

His rich laughter circled around her. "Ah, so it's *games* you don't like. Well, Brittany." His fingers moved in slow circles on her shoulder. "You won't have to *play* it. All you need to do is tug things out of your memory for me and help me collect and sort through the information. Be there when I get stuck, when I need you . . ."

Brittany's head hurt from trying to concentrate on his words instead of on the growing warmth that was dancing through her body, pinpricking up and down her arms and legs. Why did his simple, straightforward words sound like a proposition instead of a plain business deal? Where was that fine-honed finesse-with-men she'd cultivated so carefully over the past few years? She was just tired. The long day . . . the birthday party at the senior citizens home . . . She needed to get home, that was all, and settle down with a glass of warm milk. Damn, why didn't he take his hand off her shoulder?

His hand dropped to his side, but his smiling eyes remained fixed on her face.

She shivered. So, he read minds as well? she thought. Cheap parlor trick, that was all.

Sam felt her shiver and fought to keep his hands still. Shivers needed warming. . . .

Brittany backed toward the door. "I really do have to leave now." She looked around the room. Sara and Michael were lost in each other, and Gordie had slipped out unnoticed.

Her mother hadn't moved, just sat erect in the regal chair, her eyes half-closed, her gracious smile in place. As for Sam Lawrence, Brittany opted not to look. She walked briskly over to her mother and kissed her gently on the cheek. "I'm sorry, Mother, but I really do have to leave. The car . . ." She gestured vaguely toward the front of the house and the wide circle drive. "It's chilly—and they're all out there in the van. Spike and Dunkin. Oh, and Harry . . ."

She felt a hot blush coat her neck and creep upward until it covered her face.

"Harry?" Sam asked.

"A rabbit. Lop-eared," she said quickly, then edged back toward the door.

"Brittany dear." Katherine's voice was so soft she could have been speaking in her sleep.

Brittany stopped at the edge of the fringed Oriental carpet and drew in a lungful of air. She was doomed.

She turned slowly and looked into her mother's soft gray eyes. She could hear the words before they were murmured.

"It's for your father, dear, and will mean so much." Katherine patted her daughter's arm. "I knew I could count on you. I always can, Brittany."

Brittany didn't trust herself to pause, nor to look at Sam Lawrence, nor to say good-bye. Her head spinning for reasons she didn't begin to understand, she planted one more kiss on her mother's forehead, nodded her terse agreement, and picked up her oversized purse.

Sam leaned over the back of a gold brocade Queen Anne chair and watched as a battered sneaker, a huge bottle of calcium pills, and a bright blue dog collar tumbled out of the cavernous bag and onto the floor. But all he saw of consequence was the lovely light in Brittany Winters's startling eyes. A surge of adrenaline shot through him as he watched her scoop up the scattered items and stuff them back into the purse. As he straightened up, just about the time Brittany disappeared through the door, Sam realized he wasn't tired anymore. He felt quite alive as a matter of fact.

Feeling her gaze on him, he glanced over at Katherine Winters.

Her eyes were twinkling merrily. "Well, Mr. Lawrence, I do believe we have primed the pump!"

He grinned. "I think you're right, Mrs. Winters."

The tiny woman accepted his hand and let him help her from the chair. "I also believe, young man, that with the slightest bit of gentle persuasion, Brittany Ellsbeth will move over into our camp directly and be a more willing accomplice than she seemed tonight."

Sam took his jacket from a butler who appeared out of nowhere. "I hope you're right. You know your daughter far better than I do." He moved toward the door, then paused as he mulled over Mrs. Winters's words. A little friendly persuasion? That shouldn't be too difficult a task. . . . When he turned back, Katherine Winters was standing in the same spot, a knowing smile playing across her face.

A lovely woman, Katherine Winters, he thought, then waved good night and slipped through the butler-held door and out into the night.

Two

Sam heard the door click shut behind him and shrugged his jacket into place. Perhaps if he had time to talk to Brittany alone, he could lure a more willing sparkle into those lovely green eyes. He looked around the wide circular drive, lit now by tiny low lights that flickered against the black New England night. At the far end, just where the driveway emptied into the street, he spotted taillights turning right. Without a second thought he jumped into his orange VW Rabbit and gave serious pursuit.

In seconds Sam realized that what he was following was a rather used van. He squinted hard to see the driver. It couldn't be . . . not in a muddy van . . . But a pause at the first red light two blocks down the road confirmed that it was indeed Brittany Winters. He grinned and shook his head. It was like watching a Polaroid picture emerge from the black film paper. With each passing minute Brittany came into clearer focus, with more defined lines and shades and hues. What they all added up to, Sam didn't begin to guess. But she was definitely as intriguing as any game he'd had yet to figure out.

If she knew he was following her, she gave no indication. The light changed and the scratched van headed south.

She drove carefully, Sam observed, but at a healthy clip. With one hand on the wheel he leaned an elbow against the window frame and ran his fingers through his thick hair, his brows drawn together thoughtfully. Why did she resist his games? Or was it helping *him* that gave her problems? Well, he'd simply have to sit her down and explain that *he* was safe and harmless, the *game* would be brilliant, she'd love working with him, and—who knows?—they might even become friends.

Just then, as both vehicles obediently stopped for a red light, Brittany unexpectedly rolled down her window, stuck her head out, and stared at his small car.

He nodded in recognition and lifted a hand in greeting but quickly dropped it to avoid the arrows her look was spearing straight at him. For an endless moment she stared at him. Then, as the light was just turning yellow, he saw the flash of a smile in a cloud of auburn hair, and she stepped on the gas and sped across the intersection.

He followed, his foot pressing down heavily on the gas pedal. He shook his head and grinned lopsidedly. Hell, he hadn't chased fire engines in fifteen years!

She leaned around the next corner and skidded into an alleyway.

He followed.

Crazy, he thought, as stones spun beneath his wheels. Getting Brittany Winters's home address would be as difficult as finding sand in a desert. Why the hell was he doing this? He could call her tomorrow, discuss the whole game matter in a way that would charm her into willing acquiesence, and get things rolling. He could . . .

It was when he let his mind wander to more practical things that Sam got himself in trouble. As he pulled onto the main street, he spotted Brittany's van ahead, and with a surge of renewed purpose he shot after her, not giving a thought to the fact that she had slowed to a respectable twenty-five miles per hour.

The circling red light came out of nowhere.

"Oh, damn." Sam moaned as he pulled slowly over to the side of the street. He rolled down his window and shot his license out to the imposing-looking officer. "Dangerous speed, mister. Why, if there'd been traffic"—he looked up and down the deserted street—"coulda been trouble."

Sam mumbled an indecipherable answer, then looked beyond the policeman to the van that had made a U-turn and was cruising slowly past them. Brittany lifted her hand, curling her fingers in a soft wave, and continued on down the street.

He watched her until the van was a dot in the darkness, then faced the policeman with a crooked smile on his face.

The officer looked at him curiously. "Most people don't react quite so nicely, fella. They're all full of excuses about how this or that is broken and they really didn't mean to, or the wife is sick at home or havin' a baby or what have you." He flashed Sam a grin and slapped the ticket into his hand.

"No, sir. I was speeding all right. No argument there." And she'd coaxed him into it, he thought, that lovely lady who seemed so soft and vulnerable back in the plushness of the family home. His smile broadened. "Is there a phone around here?"

"Around the corner at the 7-Eleven. Now, you be careful, you hear?" The officer sauntered back to his car, leaving Sam alone to consider his next move. He scratched his chin absently as thoughts of Brittany played across his mind. He felt like a kid again, playing hooky from school and following rainbows. Damned if he didn't feel good!

The phone book was in shreds and Brittany's number was unlisted according to the efficient-voiced operator, but it took only two phone calls for Sam to get what he needed, then he was back on the road, headed north toward a quiet residential area. As he pulled onto a tree-lined street with lovely old homes, the streetlights turned from harsh neon to muted gaslights and soft shadows fell lazily across the silent pavement. He scanned the large three-story houses, then glanced down at the scribbled address on a piece of paper. Five fifty-five *a* Elery Lane. Well, he mused, admiring the stateliness of the old, well-kept homes, Brittany definitely didn't deny herself plush quarters! Five fifty-five loomed up from behind a copse of old oak trees, its gabled roof and pillared porch visible through the leafless branches. But the address he was looking for was 555*a*. Where the hell was that?

And then he saw the small post beside the driveway, a tasteful wrought-iron rectangle with an arrow and a "555*a*" raised from the surface to beckon visitors down the long brick drive that wound behind the main house. Sam followed, his senses fully tuned and his mind lit with curiosity.

Several hundred yards behind the house was a brick and wood carriage house, set like a plaything beside the massive main structure. An expanse of lighted, sashed windows stretched across the second floor and a stairway to the side offered entry.

Sam parked the car and climbed the stairs.

He glanced at the name beside the door. B. E. Winters. Right place. Now, if his luck held, the door wouldn't be opened by a man. He decided to take his chances and knocked.

It wasn't a man, but the black nose of a large, floppy-looking dog that poked through the crack in the door. Finally it opened wider and Brittany stood in the doorway, a soft fleecy robe pulled tightly around her, her eyes wide. "What . . ." she sputtered, "what in heaven's name are *you* doing here?"

He leaned against the doorframe, one foot firmly in

place should the door suddenly be closed. "You owe me thirty-five dollars for that speeding ticket, Ms. Winters." His eyes flashed. "And just for the record, it was damn foolish of you to open this door without first asking who was out here!" Standing there like that with her hair loose and free . . . and that robe inviting the eye to look beneath! Why, she'd stir the insides of a monk!

"You're absolutely right about the latter! As for the ticket— "

"You set me up. You knew that cop was there!"

She smiled almost shyly, rubbing her arms as a chill wind whipped around Sam's lanky frame. "You can lead a horse to water . . . Perhaps you shouldn't drive so fast."

He stepped in before she could stop him and leaned back against the door, snapping it closed. The reddish-brown dog smelled his pants leg, then settled down between them.

"Ms. Winters, you and I have some business to settle. Now"—he looked over her shoulder, then half-smiled into her surprised face—"shall we talk here in this drafty hallway, or warm ourselves before that fire that I see in the next room?"

The dog thumped a large hairy tail on the floor.

Brittany glared at it. "Dunkin, be quiet!" She looked back at Sam and took a step away from him. "I don't have anything to talk to you about." Her heart began to beat erratically and she wondered briefly if she was going to be sick. She was hot and cold at the same time, and her palms tingled within her clenched fists. She put one hand on the doorknob, but Sam was already walking down the hall and into the firelit room. She stiffened her back and quickly followed. "Mr. Lawrence, it's not a good time for business—" Even before Sam interrupted, she knew the words sounded faint and strangely void of purpose.

"I didn't know carriage houses had fireplaces," he

said. He shrugged out of his jacket and angled his long body down onto the plump-pillowed couch in front of the fire. He looked around the room at the thriving plants that seemed to be everywhere and the comfortable, tasteful furniture. "This is nice, very cozy." Dunkin licked his hand, then settled down on the hearth. "And you have a great dog, Brittany."

Brittany was silent.

"Here. There's room." He eyed the empty space on the small couch and extended a hand. "You look cold."

She moved out of his reach and stood near the edge of the mantel, her thoughts a fragmented mess. She didn't know whether she needed to be warmed or chilled or both. All she knew for sure was that Sam Lawrence confused her and made it difficult to think straight.

"All right, Mr. Lawrence. Since you're here, let's settle this business quickly. I'm very tired. If it's the thirty-five dollars you're after, you'll have to take me to court."

Sam watched her as his body soaked in the warmth from the fire. The light seemed to shimmer around her, clearly outlining the curving lines of her body and turning her hair into a halo of fiery auburn-gold. His breath caught in his throat. She looked so young, a raw beauty who didn't seem to fit well anyplace he'd seen her thus far: her parents' house, the rusty van. Maybe she fit here, in this cozy den of a house with a blazing fire and soft, comfortable furniture that looked used and friendly.

"Well?" she asked. She tightened the sash on her robe and looked at him steadily. "What's it to be, sir, court? Or are you going to admit thirty-five dollars is a cheap price to pay for following and harassing an innocent woman?" She smiled slightly, a small dimple appearing in her right cheek.

Progress, Sam thought. "I concede, Brittany. Sorry for the chase, I'll pay my due restitution . . . this time. But you still owe me at least an explanation—"

"I don't like to be followed."

"An explanation for your less than enthusiastic response to the game for your father." He combed his hands roughly through his hair and looked around the room, then focused back on Brittany and smiled crookedly. "I'm not used to being turned down."

"It doesn't really matter what I think, Mr. Lawrence—"

"Sam."

"Sam. Because, as you well know, the game will happen."

He leaned over and scratched Dunkin's ear. "Hmmm."

"So, you see," she continued, "there was no reason for you to follow me, to raise your car insurance rates, to climb my steep stairs, now, was there?"

When he looked up, his eyes, she saw, were filled with silent laughter. Not at all the eyes of a man who had made a wasted trip. "I'd love a brandy," he said. Dunkin nuzzled his hand to encourage another scratch.

She shook her head in surprise, but walked into the hall, relieved to escape him for a brief moment. Standing on tiptoe, she pulled a squat bottle of Courvoisier from the highest shelf of the glass-fronted hall cabinet, then rummaged around until she found two brandy snifters. She nibbled intently on her bottom lip and considered the man settling in on her sofa.

She was at ease around men, and had a comfortable number of male friends. And she had worked with many male civic leaders while raising money for Petpals. Being a member of a well-connected, socially prominent family, she never went wanting for escorts and invitations, even though she often opted to skip the more visible social events. But Sam Lawrence was unlike any of the men she'd known, and there'd been only one other who had even come near to having such a startling effect on her. And David was so far buried in her past, he didn't count anymore.

She placed the glasses and bottle on a small oval tray and turned back to the living room. Sam Lawrence was something altogether new, she mused. And she couldn't put her finger on the reason why, so she couldn't begin to handle it in her careful and effective way. And that bothered her considerably.

Be careful, Brittany, she cautioned herself, and walked back into the fire-warmed room.

Sam was standing at the fireplace, intently examining the dozens of snapshots displayed in small ornate frames.

"My rogues' gallery," she said, and laughed self-consciously.

"Nice. Very nice. The Winters clan is a very handsome one. This must be your father." He held up a framed photo of Katherine and Gordon Winters, their arms comfortably wound around each other. In the background was an old two-story house with elaborate, ornate features. "Ah, in Brussels, I'd guess."

She set the tray down on a small coffee table and walked over to look more closely at the picture. "Yes, I think it was. They went to Belgium and Wales that summer—and I especially liked that picture of them." When she looked at it a second time, her expression changed from the softness of nice memories to one of surprise. "But how did you know? There's just a tiny part of a house showing and it's mostly door. There have to be a thousand spots in Europe that look similar."

Sam grinned. "I remember things like that. Shapes and relationships linger in this thick head. For fun and profit, I did a photo study of European doors one summer."

"Doors?"

"Uh-huh. I added some text and put it all together in a book. Doors can be fascinating, and the ones in Brussels are especially so."

She smiled to encourage him to continue.

"They tell stories, welcome you, or shut you out. But they're not silent, generic rectangles. They speak to you in wonderful old crooning voices." His strong hands moved through the air as he spoke, fashioning it into shapes and images.

"How nice. I'd never thought about doors quite like that." She crossed her arms and watched him carefully.

He nodded toward the picture, a half smile softening the line of his jaw. "When you tune in to them, you discover wonderful things. It's kind of nice—an introduction to the folks who live there. We don't take time for that kind of craft much anymore. Too bad, really."

"Yes . . ." Brittany murmured, enjoying the rich sound of his voice spinning such nice thoughts. She shoved away the feelings of hurrying him out the door . . . just for a moment.

"Ever been to Europe, Brittany?"

The spell was broken. She nodded, her eyes focusing on the leaping flames of the fire.

"Where?"

"Nowhere special. London, Paris."

Sam swallowed his smile when he glanced down and read the sadness in her eyes. Traveling to far-off places was a delicious panacea for him, refreshing fuel for his mind. For Brittany, it must have been something far different. "Well," he said gently, "perhaps you were simply with the wrong person."

Her gaze remained fixed on the flickering orange flames that danced off the bricks, leaving eerie shadows cavorting around the room like live jesters. "The brandy," she said absently. "It's there on the table."

"So it is." He moved to the table and poured the Courvoisier into the two glasses, then sank back onto the comfortable couch and motioned for her to join him.

The brandy slid down her throat easily, loosening the tense feeling around her heart and behind her eyes. She settled back into the soft cushions and faced him, her smile back in place. "Now, Sam, about this game for my father . . ."

"Yes. About that game." He lifted one arm over the back of the sofa and rested his fingers inches from her head. "Help me to understand why a lovely woman like you doesn't want to help me with a gift for her own father."

His husky voice wasn't helping. She shook her head and tried to be annoyed. "I already told you why. But it doesn't matter. What matters now is that my family has offered my services to you— "

One brow rose.

"Oh, you know very well what I mean!" She dipped her head quickly to hide the blush and fumbled for her brandy snifter. "I simply don't have time to spend on this . . . this project. I really don't. Sara has more time. Or my brother."

Her emerald eyes flashed with tiny specks of gold, and her flushed face was framed in a soft mass of wavy hair. He watched as she lifted her hand to drink the brandy. The fleecy purple robe pulled tight against her firm breasts. He swallowed hard around the knot forming in his throat. He took a quick drink of brandy and continued.

"But according to everyone, Brittany, you're the one with the memories, the perception I need."

His nearness was suddenly taking away air she badly needed. "But, Sam . . ."

His fingers closed the space between them and dropped gently onto her shoulder.

She stared at his hand. "What is that?" She fought in vain to keep her voice smooth and calm.

"That is my hand touching you in a friendly gesture." Warmth spilled from his brown eyes and landed somewhere inside her. She bit down hard on her lip.

"I want only a little of your time, your help," he said. "I don't want to cause problems for you—"

She lowered her head. She *was* being foolish, and she *was* the best person to help him. She knew it, and he knew it, and her family knew it. Then why was her mind sending up flares of warning? Why couldn't she be more reasonable about this? Was it a fear that Sam would get too close to *her* life in the process? That he would loosen the dust over things best buried and forgotten?

Or was it simply Sam—and the fact that in a very short amount of time spent together, he had made her desire him—and it had nothing to do with games or work or reason!

She didn't realize he'd covered her hand with his own until she tried to wave it through the air as she spoke. It didn't move.

"Sam, I—"

She finally managed to untangle her hand, but it was too late. His long body had gradually shifted until it was as close to hers as the heat of the fire, his breath a soft, tantalizing breeze on her cheek.

Then slowly, gently, he kissed her, covering her lips with a sweet pressure that stopped her breath and drained the strength from her limbs in an instant.

She moaned silently, but was unable to move an inch as his arm curled around her back and gathered her close, his fingers separating and closing on the material of her robe just beside her breasts. Her mind was fading away, her heart doing aerobics, and her lips parted slowly as she tasted the wonder of his kiss.

She might have stayed there forever, wrapped in that delicious warmth, except she couldn't breathe at all and Dunkin was nuzzling his wet nose into her lap curiously.

"Oh . . ." She pulled back and slowly opened her eyes. She focused on Dunkin and patted his head, then looked up at Sam. In a quick, purposeful movement, she scooted as far to the end of the couch as possible and cleared her throat. "Well, I suppose that's one way of insuring cooperation, Mr. Lawrence. But let's not be silly about this."

His eyes never left hers and a slow smile lit his face as he shook his head. "That, dear Brittany, was not silly, it was wonderful. And it wasn't an insurance policy of any kind."

"What was it then?"

"It was a very sensuous, lovely kiss between two people who were *both* enjoying it like hell!"

Brittany sat stiffly. It wasn't a lovely kiss at all. A "lovely kiss" wouldn't leave her feeling so unglued—and filled with the desire to dig her hands into his hair and continue what he'd begun for an indeterminate amount of time. The "sensual" she'd grant him.

He continued. "You're a very attractive woman, you know. And I guess with the fire and the brandy and all, it seemed like a good idea. . . ."

"Well, I don't think so, not at all." She stood up and tried to stomp to the fireplace, but her huge, furry slippers turned the stomp into a muted floppy sound. Sam smiled at her movements, suddenly touched by a vulnerability that Brittany was trying too damned hard to hide. She'd been so lovely to touch, so soft and warm in his arms. . . .

He pushed himself off the couch and walked over to her, reaching out to touch her shoulder gently. "Brittany, I'm sorry. Not sorry I kissed you, that'd be a bold-faced lie. It was a wonderful kiss, in fact. But I didn't mean to offend you."

Brittany slipped from beneath his touch and circled around the back of the couch with Dunkin in intrigued pursuit. Sam Lawrence was slipping into her life, she thought. She could feel it as surely as she could feel the beat of her heart. He was bewitching her, beguiling her, and heaven only knew what else. But he didn't *fit* in her life. She knew it as surely as she knew she wanted to kiss him again.

"We need some rules, Sam."

"For playing ring-around-the-couch? That shouldn't be too diffi—"

"For getting this 'game' finished. There are some very basic things you need to know."

He lifted his brows, grinned, and settled back down on the couch.

Brittany plunged in, her eyes focusing on a point just beyond his right ear. "First off, no more come-ons like that. I don't intend to get involved with you . . . that way . . ." She snuck a look at him. He was smiling. "I mean it, Sam." At least part of her meant it, she thought. And the other part wasn't making sense. . . .

Sam nodded solemnly. Any game player worth his salt knew rules were meant to be broken. "Next rule."

"I really *do* have a job. And I *won't* let it slide by the wayside for this game. I simply won't." Her eyes sparked with determination now.

He caught the sparks and reveled in them. "Of course not," he said soothingly. "I wouldn't expect that. You shouldn't shortchange *your* job for my job."

"Yes. I mean no, I shouldn't. And I won't. That's firm."

"Right, firm." He nodded again. "And it's no problem, Brittany, because the only equipment I need in the beginning stages of a game is a yellow pad and plenty of pencils. I'll just tag along—"

"Tag along?"

"Sure. We can talk as you work. When does your day start?"

"Oh, *early*. Very, very early." *Tag along?* She looked down at Dunkin for help. He was sound asleep, his head dropped comfortably on Sam's left boot. "Much too early for a businessman, I'm afraid."

"Try me. How early?"

"I usually begin the day at the veterinarian clinic about seven." Her concentration began to falter as her gaze fell on the shadow of a beard shading his strong, square chin. He was a . . . very . . . sexy . . . man. Only great effort kept her hand from moving of its own volition to stroke the dark dusting of whiskers.

"Seven o'clock is perfect," he said. "I can get a short run in before breakfast and meet you at the clinic." He stood and rotated his shoulders slowly. "This is great. See, Brittany, it wasn't so difficult, was it? We've laid down the rules, and now we're off and running. You'll share your life—your father's life—with me, I'll help you, and in between everything else, maybe you and I can become friends. Who knows, maybe we'll come up with a game about a beautiful woman named Britt—"

"You're a dreamer, Sam Lawrence." She laughed now and found it fenced off the more unmanageable emotions. "Don't push your luck."

He shook his head and held her still with the intensity of his look. "I don't push luck, Brittany. It simply saunters right along with me, usually. If not, I go out and find it. But today, I'd have to say, it seems to have swept me directly off my feet."

He didn't touch her, but the husky richness beneath his words was more intimate than an embrace. Brittany held her smile steady. "Good night, Sam. I guess I'll see you in the morning. But let me warn you, I won't have time to concentrate. You'll have to take what you can get. And it might not be much."

He laughed, undeterred. "My whole life's a risk, Brittany. Don't you worry about a thing." He shrugged back into the jacket and headed for the door.

"Sam?"

With one hand on the doorknob he looked back into the softly lit room. "Yes, Brittany?"

"Those rules . . . I mean it. I'm not comfortable with this whole thing, with someone looking into our lives. It's not like that, you know. Life. It's not really a game."

She was wrong there, he thought. Life *was* a game in a way. You played it hard, explored all its wonderful facets. But he knew this wasn't the time to get philosophical with Brittany Winters. He nodded, touched two fingers to his forehead in a friendly salute as he said good night, and stepped out into the cold.

The sky was inky black, studded with starlight. He stood there for a minute, his hands stuffed into the pockets of his jacket. He picked out the Pleiades and counted its stars slowly. It was a perfect night for getting his telescope out.

His gaze shifted to Orion and the two tiny pinpoints of light that blinked off the Hunter's shoulders. Then he noticed it, the moon hanging against the velvety blackness, clearly visible in the winter night, with only a thin illumination circling its muted blue surface. A clear, bigger-than-life blue moon, its wrinkled face looking back at him quizzically. Sam pulled his collar up to his ears and stared back for a minute, then matched the moon's creviced smile with one of his own.

Peering out the tiny window beside the door, Brittany could see Sam standing against the blackness, his breath rising in feathery swirls in the cold air. His broad shoulders were pushed back. And for a minute she thought she heard faint music, a deep voice humming an old song—"Blue Moon."

She couldn't remember the words, so she moved silently to the door and opened it a crack.

But when she peered out, it was silent and Sam was gone. Only a blue moon, hanging ominously low, looked down at her.

Three

Brittany pulled her hair back into a pony tail and ignored the hundreds of tiny curls that escaped the band, slipped into a comfortable pair of old blue jeans and a heavy knit sweater, and headed for the O'Malley Animal Clinic, nestled directly in the heart of Windermere, Maine.

It didn't matter that she hadn't slept much the night before, had tossed and turned in the moon-bred shadows of her room, because she had everything back in order now. Her emotions were in check, her perspective on the day was fresh, and she was ready for work.

The fact that Sam was exploring the Winters family still bothered her, on principle if nothing else. Her life was private. But it was her father Sam was interested in, after all, and she'd see to it that that's where his interest stayed.

And as for the man himself, well, he had caught her off guard, plain and simple. And it certainly wasn't his fault he sent her hormones into orbit. It was a purely physical attraction. Probably. And she could certainly deal with that.

But as she walked through the friendly, freshly painted clinic that had been a second home to her for nearly two years now, the resolve born in the shadowy darkness of her bedroom the night before began to weaken. "I should have simply taken the day off and gone to his office," she muttered. "It would have worked better, certainly, and—"

"Grumbling? Before the day has even begun?" Dr. Frank O'Malley sauntered into the room carrying a clipboard and wearing that wonderful broad smile that had endeared Brittany to the gray-haired veterinarian the very first time they met.

"Oh, Doc, I'm sorry. I must have been talking to myself."

"Scolding yourself, I'd say." He let his thick glasses slip clear down to the end of his nose, where they rested comfortably. "Now, that's no way to begin the mornin', my dear. Here you go." He picked up a steaming cup of coffee from a small table near the door, poured a heaping portion of thick cream into it, and wrapped her cold fingers around it. "This'll help. Far too early for whiskey or I'd put a dab of that in to help coax a smile back to that beautiful face."

She half-smiled and took a tentative sip of the coffee while she walked over to the counter. She looked out the window, then walked back again.

Dr. Frank settled his short lumpy frame behind the desk and studied her over the rim of his glasses. "So, my lovely heiress, what's on the schedule for today and what pulls you from beneath the downy quilts an hour early?"

She glanced at the schedule she'd plucked from the desk and tapped her fingers briskly on the desktop. "Lots to do today, Dr. Frank. Thought maybe I'd get a head start. Some of the Petpals animals need baths. And I've made out a list of those that need your attention."

He groaned good-naturedly. "I could close down my own practice and work full-time keeping this Petpals outfit going."

She threw him a grin. "Well, why not? You know you get just as much satisfaction out of this as I do!"

When she had approached Dr. Frank with the idea of starting Petpals a couple of years ago, he'd jumped right in, helping her put together a trust to fund it, finding wealthy donors, and providing an office for her above his back kennels. It was a delightful enterprise for both of them: she could leave her old job with Trust and Foundations and throw herself into something that involved direct contact with people every day, and he had the satisfaction of helping bring some sunlight to the folks at the rest homes.

She glanced at Dr. Frank and saw he was looking keenly at her.

"What's on your mind today, love?" he asked.

"Oh, this and that," she hedged.

"Does the *that* have anything to do with the urgent messages your lovely mother kept leaving with me yesterday about you being on time for a family get together?"

"You know my mother." Brittany leafed through the papers, jotting down brief notes that said nothing. She attached her anxiousness to the note-taking, to the day's schedule, to the dogs that needed vaccinations. And only finally, when the front door breezed open with a windy, swishing sound, to Sam Lawrence.

She spun around.

"Hmmm, too early for patients," Dr. Frank said as he pulled himself from the chair.

"Oh, I guess I forgot to tell you—" Brittany began, but Sam's long strides brought him to the inner office before the sentence could be ended. He wore the same corduroy pants from the day before, but kept off the chill with a heavy fisherman sweater. And there was something new, she thought, glancing at his hand. He was holding a fine-grained English pipe.

"Hello," Sam said. He smiled at Brittany, his gaze lingering, enjoying the tilt of her head, the natural blush that marked the graceful curve of her cheekbones, the snug fit of her jeans. She was less refined, more earthy today. And the casual Brittany Winters was every bit as lovely as the other. Reluctantly, he turned toward the white-haired gentleman and extended his hand. "I'm Sam Lawrence. And you must be the veterinarian who handles Brittany's brood."

Frank smiled and shook his hand. "Nice to meet you. You're a friend of Brittany's?" He lifted heavy brows over his bright, hopeful blue eyes.

"Oh, no, Doc," Brittany said quickly. "Sam's been hired by my mother."

"Oh? A body guard?" Frank chuckled, and Sam joined in. "Lord knows it wouldn't be such an awful idea, as pretty a young thing as Brittany is."

It had never bothered Brittany before that, although she was nearly thirty years old, Dr. Frank still had trouble allowing her to leave her teens. Today it irritated her.

She slapped her notebook down on the desk and attempted to take control. "Not a bodyguard at all, Dr. Frank. Mr. Lawrence is a . . . a . . ." Lord, what *did* you call someone who made games about people anyway?

"Game designer," Sam said with a broad smile, tapping the air with his pipe. "At least for today."

"Well, now, that's great!" Frank pumped Sam's hand harder.

"Sam's doing some work for Dad's company. And Mother wants me to help him with some information. That's all."

"Well, that's just fine," Frank said."You run along and take the day off, Brittany, and I'll have the receptionist call the senior citizens homes and have them reschedule your visit."

"Oh, no, Doc!" Brittany said.

"No, please," Sam agreed solemnly. "You see, Dr. O'Malley— "

"Frank."

Sam grinned. "Well, Frank, Brittany and I have an agreement that she'll help me as long as she can carry out her job, which is only fair, after all. I'll just follow along and gather what information I need, Brittany will do her thing, and everyone will be happy."

"Fine arrangement," Dr. Frank agreed. "The folks miss her and the menagerie when she doesn't show, you know. Those pets help put some life back into the long days. And Brittany here does a damn fine job of it. She's the best."

Brittany brushed aside his praise and handed Dr. Frank her list of things to do. "These are the Petpals animals who need checkups. The rest I'm taking with me."

"With *us,*" Sam said.

She eyed him warily. "Are you sure you're up to this? I'll understand if you choose to go back to your office. I can meet you there later."

Sam noticed the tinge of hopefulness that laced her words. "Not on your life, lovely lady. Natural settings, casual tête-à-têtes—that's where I find the meat for my games. I'm looking forward to today."

Dr. Frank leaned back in his worn leather chair and smiled at the two of them as Brittany shrugged into her jacket and headed wordlessly for the door. Sam was only an inch or two behind. "It's a great day, you know," he philosophized to their backs. "The fusion of autumn and winter, a time to—"

Brittany spun around and stared at him, a tiny smile pulling at the edges of her mouth. "Dr. Frank, what are you trying to say?"

He smiled and lifted one shoulder, then looked at Sam, who had also turned. "Say, do you play chess, Sam?"

"Sure do."

Dr. Frank nodded slowly, a pleasant, knowing grin spread across his wide face. "I thought so. We'll have to play, you and I. Now, off with you both. And have a grand day." He pushed his glasses back in place and leaned forward across his desk, shuffling papers.

Brittany looked at him for a moment, then shook her head resignedly and walked out the door with Sam a heartbeat behind.

Sam helped Brittany load her animals, then settled into the lumpy front seat of her van and checked over his shoulder for possible loose animals. All except Dunkin were confined in small cages, with rabbits and kittens sharing habitats, and multicolored puppies yelping from behind silver grids.

"Fasten your seat belts, pals," he cautioned them. "Looks like we're ready to launch."

With a lurch Brittany pulled the van out of the gravel parking lot and out onto the main thoroughfare. She often had company on Petpals visits, she thought. A fair number of volunteers from the local community came on a regular basis. So shape up, she scolded herself silently, and stop acting as if this is unusual. Treat this for what it is: a rather unorthodox business meeting.

"You're going to have to ask me questions, I suppose," she murmured, her eyes focusing on the road. "I'm not very good at coming up with things to talk about."

Sam examined her profile carefully, her soft words lingering between them. She tried to smile away the hesitancy in her voice, and when she did, he noticed the dimples that appeared on each side of her mouth. Something stirred inside him, and he fought the urge to touch those dimples, to trace the slight curve of her lips as they turned into a smile. Instead, he pulled a brown paper bag out of his briefcase and slipped it into her lap.

"Don't worry about talking, or questions," he said. "It'll all come when it should. Here, this is for you."

She looked down at the package for a second, then back at the road. "What's this?"

"A gift for letting me impose on your day like this."

When she stopped at a red light, she opened the bag and pulled out a large hardcover book. The fine glossy cover pictured a beautiful walnut door set against a pure white background. The title, *Come In*, was printed in beautiful script down the side. "Oh, Sam, this is the photo study you mentioned."

"Pure coffee table stuff, but fun."

"It's beautiful! So you really are an author."

"I take pictures. The doors speak for themselves. They really didn't need me to write much about them."

She ran her fingers over the smooth cover, admiring the purity of the photo. "A photographer," she said softly. "And a game designer. And I wonder what else you are?"

The words were spoken almost to herself, but Sam picked up on the question and sat back in the seat, his fingers laced behind his head, smiling as he mulled it over. "Hmmm, that's a toughie. A dreamer, I guess, a romantic. Someone born in the wrong century my mother used to tell me."

"Oh? Were you too early or too late?"

"Well, Madeline Lawrence, bless her, thought perhaps I would have been happier earlier in time."

"The ancient Greeks, perhaps?" Brittany could easily see him as a Grecian scholar, white robe draped dramatically over that wonderful body. . . .

He laughed. "Well, Renaissance, actually, although I've also been accused by that same lady of living with one foot stuck in tomorrow." He shrugged charmingly.

Brittany nodded. Yes, she could see that too. Sam Lawrence was a Renaissance man of sorts. So very, very appealing. Yes she knew about restless dreamers. . . .

Sam noticed her pensive look. "A penny for your thoughts." Instinct compelled him to smooth away the mood before it rooted. "I know. You're falling asleep listening to my life story, that's it. And I can't blame you a bit."

"No, no, Sam. I have a feeling your life is very interesting. Tell me, does your mother live here in Maine?" A blaring horn behind her told her the light had changed and she shifted the van into first gear.

Sam shook his head. "She died a few years ago, not long after my father. They lived their life together in a tiny twenty-square-mile area—going together to the store, their church, the VFW club. And my father going to the post office, where he worked. Their whole existence was wrapped up tightly in those few blocks. After he died, my mother's life was so shattered and she missed him so much, she wanted to join him."

Brittany nodded. She'd often thought the same would happen to her own parents, should one lose the other.

"But to tell you the truth, Brittany, I'd much rather hear about *you*." He rested one hand casually on the seat back, his fingers falling idly onto her shoulder. "After all, that's why I'm here."

"To hear about my father," she said quickly.

"Right." He shifted in his seat, amused by the sudden knowledge that he'd talk about shelling peas if it meant sitting here alongside Brittany. "Okay, Gordon Winters. There's a lot to talk about there: Business mogul par excellence. Windemere's Man of the Year. Listen, Brittany, I've been doing some reading about your dad, and I've pieced together a structure I'd like to run past you. Okay with you?"

She nodded.

"Good. Tell me what you think now." He kept his one hand near her shoulder while the other moved in the air in front of them, as if parceling it out into a game board. "Except for his business, Gordon Winter's life is project-oriented. He moves from one project to another, completing each with incredible success. It's almost an art with him, as I see it. Whether it's organizing events for the Children's Hospital, or collecting those wonderful antique cars, planning things for the family, or whatever. I'd like to formulate the game around that fact. Am I on target?"

She nodded again, more enthusiastically this time. Sam was amazing, she thought, *and* insightful. "You're right, Sam. And even when he was younger, he'd plunge himself into things, forming clubs, or devoting himself to a friend's political campaign." She laughed. "And usually, the candidate he backed was the most outspoken, controversial guy around."

Sam pulled out a long yellow pad while Brittany was talking and started to jot things down. His smile was hidden as he listened and wrote. Besides delighting him by just being beside him, Brittany was going to help him create a terrific board game. And she didn't even seem aware that her opposition to the game had drifted out the window about two miles back.

She continued, her voice lifting and falling with humor and love as she spoke of her father. "He's even project-oriented with *us*, wanting us to climb up the ranks in scouts, for example." She laughed and her eyes sparkled happily. "Dad always says one of his concerns is that there're two projects he's not completed. He never became an eagle scout."

Chuckling, Sam pulled his pipe out of a pocket and tapped down the tobacco. "And . . . ?"

She shook her head and sunlight caught in the wavy, wayward strands of reddish-gold. "And the other he'll *never* give up on—to see his girls 'married and settled,' as he puts it."

"Well, Sara has begun that little project."

"Yes, and Dad's thrilled about it. He shakes his head at me, though."

"You're not the 'settling' type?" Sam watched as a thoughtful look clouded over her beautiful eyes.

"Oh, I *am*. I'll marry sometime. But it needs to be just right."

He laughed. "And what, lovely Brittany, is 'just right'?"

She shrugged. "Oh, I don't know. The essentials—

deep feeling, love. But in addition, I'll only marry someone who is very solid and dependable. Always there."

Commitment, he thought. Of course, Brittany would demand that. And deserved it. There was an unusual strength and conviction lacing her words that made it clear she'd settle for nothing less. "In other words, not a drifting dreamer, right?"

"Yes, exactly."

His fingers tapped across her shoulder playfully. "You should have told me that before I fell beneath your spell, dear Brittany."

His husky laughter wrapped around her and Brittany savored the wonderful feelings he spun there in the old van. She forced a light laugh. "Oh, Sam, I'm sure you'll survive. What are your feelings on the blessed state?"

He drew on his pipe and became serious, but she noticed laughter still lingered in his eyes. "My feelings are that it *is* a blessed state. And that I'm not among the blessed. I'll never marry."

She shot him a quick look. Beneath his crooked smile she could see he meant each word.

"No 'Que sera sera'?"

"Nope. Marriage means permanent address in a way that causes all my essential functions—breathing, heartbeat, and so forth—to cease. Strangles me."

"You've tried it?"

"No. When Socrates told me to 'know thyself,' I took him seriously. And I know what a person like me would do to another person in a dependent situation like marriage. Both parties would suffer." He smiled slowly. "But I never, *ever* talk about things like that." His fingers pressed into the soft skin of her shoulder, kneading lightly.

"Back to the game . . ." she suggested wisely.

"Yes . . . the game."

She shifted in the seat and sped on down the highway. They had gotten so personal, she and this man she suspected she should hold at bay. But what frightened her the most was the growing awareness that a part of her didn't really want to keep Sam Lawrence at bay at all.

And *that* thought was so perplexing, she almost missed the turn through the wide pillared gates of the Elms Senior Citizens Home. Only Dunkin's barking and large paw indelicately flopping over the back of the seat saved the turn.

"Dunkin, thank you," she said as she pulled the van to a stop in the wide drive.

"May I presume Dunkin has brought us to the Elms?" Sam teased. "We zipped through the gate so quickly, I missed the sign."

"Yes, this is it." She opened her door and hopped out. "And this, Sam, is my unofficial favorite among the seven or eight places we visit. I have volunteers who help with the program, but I selfishly keep this stop for myself. It was my first, and I guess I'm attached . . ."

He looked around at the wide porches and rolling green lawns. "It has a nice, friendly look about it."

"It's wonderful," she said. "I come here twice a week—sometimes more if I have time. Most of the places we visit on a semi-monthly basis, but the Elms would have us *every* day, I think, if we could fit it in. It's sort of a haven for me—saves me from ever needing an analyst. Come on, you'll see!"

Her enthusiasm was fresh and contagious, and twisted its way right into Sam. "Delighted," he said as he swung himself from the van.

Carrying cages and with Dunkin padding excitedly beside them, they climbed the wide steps to the front door.

Inside the elegant home the excitement Petpals generated floated like a refreshing mist through the freshly scrubbed hallways.

"Ah, there she is! Hello, Brittany." An elderly woman, her thin hands grasping the rungs of a walker and holding her frail body straight, moved toward them. "Where is my Piggy?"

Sam watched from behind a cage of kittens as Brittany patted the elderly woman on the arm and quickly pulled from a cage a tiny dog with a black ring around one eye. The woman's eyes grew bright.

"Piggy's been pining away for you, Mrs. Henderson. Let's head for the lounge and find a snug place for her to settle."

The woman dutifully followed Brittany into a bright sunny room filled with comfortable chairs, plants, and half a dozen wheelchairs.

Sam watched as Brittany moved gracefully from one expectant resident to another, distributing dogs and cats into waiting, willing arms. The expression in her eyes was warm and caring, and her smile revealed her sincere affection for each person as she chatted with them.

Her gestures, he noticed with his photographer's eye, were gentle but filled with strength and conviction. She moved with a relaxed, comfortable rhythm here, where she'd carved a niche for herself.

Brittany was intriguing.

She glanced over at him and caught his look. It was far too intimate for this setting, she thought.

"Come on, Sam," she said. "We need some help with Harry and the other lop-eared rabbits." Her hands were full of Persian cat, but she motioned with a toss of her head to the remaining two cages.

"Rabbits?"

"Certainly, young man," a bald-headed man scolded from a corner. "Harry will eat from no other hands but mine, I tell you. Get him on over here."

Sam grinned and did as he was bid, carrying the lumpy rabbit to the man's chair.

"Now, sir," an elegant-looking woman on Sam's right said, "are you Brittany's young man?"

He laughed. "Well, you might say so."

Brittany glanced at him over the top of the kitten cage.

"Temporarily," he amended quickly. "We're doing some work together."

"Well, that's a fine way to get to know each other."

"Dandy, Frances," added a plump woman feeding a dog biscuit to one of the puppies. "I met Harold that way, working together. I was a sec—"

"We know, Bertha," the carefully coiffed Frances said. "What we don't know is what the young man does." She smiled sweetly at Sam while she waited for him to pull up a chair and chat over two kittens, a black puppy, and a cup of tea that was set on the small table beside him.

Sam was enchanted. Frances Sullivan was eighty-nine, claimed to have sat on the hill at Kitty Hawk the day the Wright brothers flew their first plane, and spoke with the precise articulation of an aristocrat. She'd been at the Elms three years now, she confided to him, because living alone wasn't a sane alternative at her age. She was fond of the way of life here, if only the library were strengthened and the activities more diverse. But she was working on that, she assured him with a twinkle in her eye.

When she had a free moment, Brittany watched Sam and Frances, noting the easy camaraderie and the charm that flowed so naturally from him, drawing in Frances and the other residents who had pulled up chairs and joined in the conversation.

That Sam Lawrence had never met a stranger shouldn't really be a surprise, she thought. He'd wrapped her mother around his little finger, had Frank O'Malley offering her days off, had Dunkin sleeping on his shoe. But it hadn't registered, maybe because of the thick fog that seemed to have settled around her the past twenty-four hours.

She watched him move over to Jerry Fitzgerald's chair and bit back a grin. Mr. Fitzgerald had a heart of gold beneath his aloof exterior, but he didn't often show it, nor did he take well to strangers. He'd be a challenge even to Sam Lawrence. The thought somehow tickled her.

Sam settled himself on a low settee near the elderly man's wheelchair and offered his hand. "Sam Lawrence, nice to meet you."

"Hmph." The other man glanced at him with sharp eyes, then turned back to stare out an empty doorway. "We've never met."

Sam looked up and his gaze fell on Brittany's smiling face. Her green eyes flashed with challenge. He lifted one brow, grinned back, then faced the elderly man with determination.

From the few words the man had said, Sam guessed that he had lived abroad for quite some time, and he could see from the still-prominent muscles in his legs that he'd played sports in his day. Putting those two observations together, he decided to take a chance that the man had played Rugby, a favorite sport of his.

"Say, what'd you think about that Milwaukee Rugby team?"

The old man's eyes lit up. "Wonderful! And a great sport. Kept me on my feet and agile until just a while ago." He eagerly sat forward in his chair. "I'm Jerald Fitzgerald the Third, and I'm mighty pleased to meet you."

Brittany watched them for a moment with a touch of surprise, then shook her head and turned to rescue a tiny kitten that was burrowing beneath the chair cushion. It was silly to be troubled that Sam fit in so well, she told herself.

"Okay, Sam," she said an hour later as she approached him and Jerry Fitzgerald. The two men were heatedly discussing the British empiricists and the best curve of a pipe stem. "We need to gather the animals."

Sam artfully ended the conversation with a promise to continue it later, then stood and walked over to her.

One of his arms naturally encircled her shoulders. "You sound a little brusque, Brittany."

She shook her head. "Of course not. But there are things to do, that's all."

He tugged gently on her pony tail and gazed into her eyes. "Something's bothering you."

Of course there was, she thought. And it made about as much sense as high school physics had. She liked Sam Lawrence a whole lot. Her friends here liked him a whole lot. And it bothered her enormously for reasons that circled around inside her mind but made no rational sense. "No, Sam. It's just that—"

"That you don't want me too close. *And* you're surprised I like it here so much because you didn't think my world extended much farther than winning at Monopoly."

"I—I didn't know you won at Monopoly," she mumbled.

His face softened. "I don't; I lose. Or fall asleep. I never seem to get past Go. I lose at my own games too. But I usually win at what's important." He moved closer, and when he spoke again his breath feathered the fine hairs on her neck. "Don't be upset about surprises we find in each other, Brittany. Surprises are good for the soul."

"Well that's debatable, Sam. Some souls, maybe, but not this one." She forced a bright smile and bent to escape the tickling breath of his words. "Here, take Hawthorne." She thrust a tawny-colored kitten into his hands. "And this." Piggy was tucked under his arm.

Delilah, the smallest lop-eared rabbit, was the last to be retrieved. She was sleeping soundly in the folds of Betta Marie Hopper's purple sweater. And Betta Marie was sleeping just as soundly. Sam looked at the tiny woman who was slumped down in the chair. "Hmmm."

"Just lift her arm and slip Delilah out," Brittany said. "She won't even wake up."

He did as directed. The rabbit opened one eye, then fell back to sleep in the curve of his arm.

The van was packed and ready to go in two thumps of a rabbit's tail, as Sam put it, and soon they were driving back to the clinic.

Brittany was completely aware of Sam as she drove, even though he didn't say much but just scribbled on his yellow pad and puffed thoughtfully on his pipe.

"Do you think this bothers the animals?" he asked eventually, holding the pipe out in front of him.

She glanced quickly over her shoulder. The animals were quiet. "No, I don't think so."

"Does it bother you?"

"No."

"Good." He smiled and rested his head against the back of the seat. "This was a fine day, Brittany."

She looked over at him but said nothing.

"I'd like to come along again."

"Why?" she asked, her voice lifting in surprise.

"Well, lots of reasons, not the least being that I like sitting in this crowded van with you."

"And the other reasons?"

"I like that place. They're great folks. And in between times you tell me things that are interesting and useful for the game."

"I do?"

"Yep. And I also have a much stronger feeling for the Winters family as a whole by being with you, a feeling for how your father raised you, what he was like as a father, that sort of thing."

"You'd make a fine private eye, Sam Lawrence," she said with a laugh. "But somehow it's a little disconcerting to know someone is picking up on everything I say, storing it away, and doing heaven knows what with it."

"Oh, you'll know before heaven does. You're going to have to check everything. My instincts and perceptions are usually pretty much on target, or at least I like to think so, but I do need you to double-check. You're the real key to this game, Brittany."

She pulled the car into the parking lot of the clinic

and switched off the engine. And what responsibilities did being the key to the game embrace? she wondered. "Well, Sam, I guess I can handle that, as long as it's as painless as it was today."

He was still for a minute as he watched her face in the shadows of the car. He didn't want her to get out, to move away from him, and the force of the realization threw him into uncharacteristic silence.

"So . . ." She wrapped her fingers around the car keys and pulled them out of the ignition. "I guess it's fine if you want to come along to the Elms."

He nodded, and a pleasing warmth filled him at the thought of spending more days this way, wandering through Brittany's life with her. In fact, he could think of little at that moment he'd prefer.

"Sam?" She was looking at him intently. "I think it'll work fine if you want to come along."

His pensiveness disappeared and he directed his full attention to her. "Fine. We're a good pair, don't you think?"

"Well, the folks did like you, I'll admit to that."

"And you like me—better than yesterday at least."

It wasn't a question but she nodded anyway, laughing away the tightness tugging inside her. "Sure, Sam. Who wouldn't like you? You're a charmer."

"Then I haven't been too much of a pest."

She looked at his lopsided smile and shook her head. "Of course not. I've enjoyed the day."

"How much?"

"How much? If this is another game, Sam, I think I may have played it in junior high."

His hand rested on her shoulder. "No game, Brittany. I was simply wondering if you enjoyed it as much as I did."

Her heart started to pound heavily. "Well, Sam, on a scale of one to ten . . ."

His hand strayed from her shoulder up beneath the

pony tail, where he gently rubbed the tender skin on her neck. "On a scale of one to ten . . . ?"

"It was definitely at least a seven-plus day. And maybe, after I've had a chance to think it through, maybe I'll give it an eight."

He nodded slowly. "I'd say an eight for sure."

His fingers were working magic on her neck and she wanted to stop talking and let herself fall into the delicious feel of his caress. "Oh, Sam, that's wonderful," she murmured. "You're heading for an eight-plus."

"Hmmm, you're easy to please, Brittany Winters." As he continued to massage her neck, his gaze wandered around the inside of the van. "I used to have a van like this when I was in high school."

"Oh?"

"It was much older and had been through several lifetimes before I inherited her, but she was dependable. I used it to deliver old Mr. Wassink's groceries to his customers."

She nodded, a slow smile curving her lips. "I see." One tiny part of her urged her to open the door and fall out into the cold, stabilizing air. But it was so tiny, so dim, that it barely mattered. And the larger part of her gave in to the enchantment, to staying and talking and enjoying the lovely feeling of Sam's fingers smoothing out the fine hair on her neck. It felt so *good.* She lifted her lids and saw the smiles that spilled from his eyes.

"Being in a van again makes me feel like a teenager," he said.

She kept her gaze on his face.

"Remember when you used to neck in a car?"

She laughed but didn't move. "Yes. Forgotten youth."

His voice grew husky. "I don't want to scare you or mess this up, Brittany, but I want more than anything right this minute to take you in my arms and kiss you. Do you know what I mean?"

It all seemed to happen in slow motion then, her dreamy, understanding nod, his sliding closer on the cold seat, his hand gently cupping her face, and then his lips hungrily covering hers with strong, persuasive passion. He pulled away once, just a fraction of an inch. She took in a quick breath of air, but was waiting when he returned, his lips pressing firmly, his tongue moving until she opened her mouth slightly and let him feed the flowering within her.

When at last he pulled away, she wasn't ready at all for the cooling distance. She took in a lungful of air and wound her fingers around the cold steering wheel. "But something's different, Sam," she said gravely.

"Different?"

"I don't have the urge to run inside to call my best friend." She managed a small grin.

"I know what you're saying. What do you think it means?"

She brushed her hair back, then rested her hand briefly on his arm. "I think it's Dr. Frank. He put some kind of a spell on us this morning with his talking about autumn and winter meshing together." She looked over toward the clinic and noticed two of the volunteers leaving the building, coming to help unload the animals.

Sam followed her gaze. "Yep, maybe that's it. Musta been. I've never been 'spelled' before. I think I like it."

She studied him closely. She liked it too. Much more than she dared admit.

"Not being very familiar with this particular type of spell," he continued, "or what the remedy is, I guess we'll just have to wait and see what happens." He reached across her and opened her door. He stayed there for a moment, his chest angled toward her breasts, his face just inches from hers. "Agreed?"

When she nodded, her forehead brushed his. "That's what we get for acting like teenagers."

He laughed as he slid back across the seat. "Maybe youth knows something we don't."

He swung his body from the van and Brittany slipped out on the opposite side. Maybe youth did, she mused.

The volunteers were already opening the back of the van and she took one more calming breath of air. Then she waved good-bye to Sam as he headed for his car. There was a caring in his eyes that wrapped around her tightly as he waved back. She knew it wasn't a spell at all. And whatever it was, she had a feeling it would be far more difficult to break.

Far more difficult.

Four

Even if it had been a spell, Brittany decided with a wonderful sense of confidence several days later, she was handling it just fine. She had no need for a cure, nor did she want one. If nothing was broken, why fix it? She accepted the days with Sam as easily as the sunshine and laughter that seemed to come with them.

Sam flirted as naturally as he breathed, but no harm was done. Everything was turning out fine, including the game, which, Sam said, was moving along at a steady clip.

And now, after two hours of traipsing through an old factory with Sam, she not only knew a lot about games, but they were both nearly experts on the fine art of umbrella-making.

"Did you really want to see how all those umbrellas were made?" she asked. She tilted her head back to catch the rays of the late afternoon sun as she and Sam emerged from the large two-story factory. A toasty warmth ran through her. It had been a good day. They'd completed their fourth day of Petpals visits, and had even managed a trip to this wonderful old factory where her father had worked so many years before.

"Those aren't just umbrellas, Brittany. Those are

umbrellas—works of art. It was fascinating, didn't you think? And the guys on the assembly line were terrific."

"And you asked enough questions to steal all their secrets and start your own company. I don't think they know quite what to make of you, Sam."

"Well, Brittany. . ." He slipped one arm around her shoulders and whispered teasingly against her cheek, "It didn't matter what they thought of me, because you were my ticket. They thought you were a present from the gods."

"Oh, Sam!" she groaned. "Don't you ever stop?"

"Nope," he answered with the same disarming smile that played havoc with her concentration at the nursing homes. "And those good men also think a great deal about one Gordon Winters. Did you catch all those tales about the days when he managed the plant?"

She nodded, her thoughts settling somewhere between his words and the nice feel of his body so close to hers.

"Well, they loved him. I especially liked that story the older gent told about him bringing in a donkey on election day."

She laughed, remembering. "And afterward he raffled it off and gave the money to some fellow who had lost nearly everything in a poker game."

"I'm surprised you didn't adopt it for Petpals."

"I wasn't born yet."

"Ah. I knew there had to be a logical reason." His laugh rippled through the crisp autumn air. "You know, Brittany, I'm looking forward to meeting your father."

"You two will get along fine. And I know he'll like the game, no matter what I said about poker."

He grinned and without a thought hugged her close, then released her just enough so they could walk along through the late afternoon shadows. "You're a pushover, you know. It's taken less than a week to make a believer out of you."

"Now don't count your chickens, Lawrence," she

said, her loose hair rubbing against the soft wool of his jacket. "I simply said he would like the game. However, he'll probably never *play* it."

They had reached Sam's small Volkswagen and he held open the door for her to get in. "Shall we wager a bet, my sweet Brittany?"

"I don't gamble, Sam." She slipped into the car and looked back up into his laughing eyes. "Sorry."

"Never?"

She kept her smile in place, but her mind slipped back over the years. Never? She had gambled once, a long time ago . . . And she had lost. But it was so very long ago. A lifetime ago . . . "Oh, I guess it depends, Sam. I'll gamble on sure winners . . . maybe."

He strode around to the other side of the car and got in next to her. "Then it's a bet." He leaned over and brushed a quick kiss across her cheek to seal it, then straightened and started the engine. "Except you're on the wrong side of the fence for this one."

Brittany scolded away the uncomfortable stirrings inside her. They were talking about games, after all. Nothing more, nothing less. And Sam was right: it was a sure winner. The game . . . nothing else . . .

"Hungry?" he asked.

He was studying her, his eyes reading deep. But his smile was so gentle, she settled back against the seat and nodded easily, the unsettling feeling beginning to vanish. "Yes."

"Good. And it's no small wonder. I've dragged you from here to kingdom come today." He reached over and playfully tickled her knee. He'd seen the look that had shadowed her smile a second ago, a distant look, and he wanted to chase it away. His fingers danced a jig on her knee. "Thanks for coming with me, Brittany."

Her heart was beating to his touch and she only smiled in answer.

"I needed you there beside me in those places." His fingers settled on her leg. "I needed you to charm those men into baring their souls—and to coax them into sifting through dusty memories. And you did it, Brittany." His husky voice deepened dramatically and he swept his hand through the air with a flourish. "You were, in a word, mag-ni-fi-cent!"

"Oh, Sam, hush. Such drama. Were you ever on the stage?"

"Always."

She laughed, and he laughed, and together the sound sparked the air until Brittany felt it beneath her skin and running through her veins.

"Now, fair maiden, what kind of gourmet masterpiece would delight you?"

"Hmmm, let me think."

When he pulled up to a stoplight, Sam looked over and noticed that she had closed her eyes. Her gold-tipped lashes rested so quietly on her skin, she could have been asleep. Waves of bronze hair tumbled loosely onto her brilliant blue turtleneck. Her breasts rose and fell rhythmically beneath the soft fabric. His breath caught. She was so damn lovely and vulnerable-looking. He'd had to fight his baser instincts for days now, and wondered if it would get easier. He doubted it.

With his eyes he traced the delicate curve of her cheekbones and the dusting of freckles across her nose. They were so temptingly sweet, he had a sudden urge to kiss each one. The thought brought a slow smile to his face and he shifted involuntarily in the seat. Ah, Brittany, he thought. Trusting, beautiful Brittany. What in the name of all that's right in the universe was she doing to him?

That same sudden shift in emotions that had been ailing him for several days came back in full force and caused a tightening between his eyebrows and a flash of warning in his head. He couldn't quite put words to the feeling, but it was Brittany—all Brittany—of that he was more than sure. It had been almost instant, the attraction he felt for her, and it burned inside of him now. He felt her presence in the darnedest places. It was Brittany he saw in the glassy surface of the river when he ran along its edge early in the morning; and it was a copper-haired beauty with a smile as fresh as daffodils who ruffled his thoughts when he considered the next few months of his life. He had no right or reason to put her there in the middle of his mind like that.

Except there she was. Brittany Ellsbeth Winters, her eyes bright, her voice edged with laughter. And the mere tilt of her head and flip of that mass of fiery-edged hair lit his desires to rival an Independence Day display.

The harsh blare of a horn behind him brought Sam's attention back to the road, but the nagging feeling remained, a relentless reminder that Brittany Winters was different, and that a friendly, amicable affair was not a part of her vocabulary. Nor should it ever be.

He switched on the radio. Easy strains of a symphony filled the car and smoothed out his thoughts until he felt comfortable and easy again.

It was Brittany who broke the silence several miles later. Sitting up straight, she looked out at the passing houses and small stores, the people on foot hurrying home from bus stops. "Sam, where are we? I've never seen this part of Windemere before." She craned her neck to glimpse a street sign in the fading light, but it only told her she was in the northeast section of town.

"What?" Sam seemed pulled from a daze. He looked around, then sucked in a long, deliberate breath. Only after a minute had passed did he allow a half smile to ease the tightness of his mouth.

The houses lining the road were as familiar to him as the back of his hand. So were the shady streets, the people hunched against the cold as they walked, and the kids in worn jeans doing wheelies on their bikes. Why had he come back here? He shook his head slowly.

"We're in Shadyside, Brittany. It's a small little co-

coon that's officially a part of Windemere but never claims that aloud. Memorial Cemetery and the Blue River separate it from the city, and Shadyside folks like that just fine."

"Shadyside . . . Of course. I've heard of it and knew it was up here somewhere. I guess I just never had occasion to come this way."

"No, probably not." He turned a corner and slowly drove down a shaded, quiet street. "And people here don't have much need to venture into the rest of Windemere. At least my parents didn't."

Brittany swiveled on the seat in surprise. "Your parents? Then this is where you grew up?"

He nodded.

She turned again to look out the window and her voice grew thoughtful. "Funny, I guess I assumed you were from somewhere else, not Windemere. I don't know why."

"Actually, I *wasn't* from Windemere. I was from Shadyside." He smiled crookedly and ran a finger over her cheek.

"Semantics," she said.

"No, truth." He gestured to the houses they were passing. "This was my family's whole world. Shadyside had everything they needed. Grocery stores, a movie theater, a couple of churches, and its own red brick VFW building, where they had meetings every Friday, bingo every Saturday, and poker for the guys on Thursday nights."

"Sam, it's a charming place."

"Homey."

"Whatever. But it *is* picturesque."

Sam turned another corner and she gazed at the rows of houses. They were all of the same vintage, one hundred years old or more, she guessed, and had the same flavor about them, as if they'd been scooped out of the same batter and dropped neatly onto the land. Small square parcels of yard were meticulously kept, and bunches of brilliantly colored marigolds and late-blooming flowers lined walkways and porches. "Sam, let's stop."

He shrugged. Hell, they were here, he thought. For what bizarre reason he could only begin to guess. Maybe he unknowingly wanted Brittany to see it all, and to understand him better through the seeing. So she'd know what he was all about, why he didn't stay put for long. Know it all, right from the start. And then again, maybe *he* wanted to figure out what he was all about . . . And then again . . .

He raked a hand roughly through his hair and laughed at himself and the tangle of thoughts vying with one another inside his head. It was a beautiful day, Brittany was beside him; what more mattered for the moment? "Okay, Brittany. Sure, why not? They even have a few eateries in Shadyside. Including one that makes the best hamburgers in the known world. You'll love it." He drove a few blocks farther and pulled over to the side of a street lined with small stores.

"Shadyside's main drag," he announced ceremoniously as they both climbed out of the car. "My parents' house was that one right off Main Street." He pointed beyond the car to a side street and Brittany spotted a neatly kept house with deep blue shutters that looked just like all the others.

Sam's house. A giant old oak tree shadowed one of the upstairs windows and she could picture him climbing its tangled branches, his blue jeans torn and a mischievous grin spreading across his youthful face.

"I used to sneak out my window and shimmy down the tree," he said, pointing, and she laughed.

"I knew that."

He looked down and grinned at her. "Oh, you did, did you? And what else do you know about me?"

"More each minute." She smiled back, her heart feeling strangely full.

His gaze lingered on her face a moment longer, then

shifted to the signs and storefronts along Main Street. He could close his eyes and picture each one with the details a child records. The peeling paint, the plants in an upstairs window, the dentist's lopsided tooth hanging proudly next to his sign.

Brittany's soft voice filtered into his memories. "Has it changed much since you lived here?" She stood close, and her shoulder gently touched his when he moved.

He looked at her and took her hand. "Changed? No, not one bit. Come on, I'll give you the grand tour."

The street was nearly empty as they walked along hand in hand, the crisp leaves crackling beneath their footsteps and the cool breath of dusk quickening their step.

"Where is everyone?" Brittany asked.

Sam glanced at the large clock that decorated the front of Christenson's Variety Store. "It's dinnertime. Everyone is home eating. In an hour or so there'll be movement again. It's Thursday night."

"Poker at the VFW. I see." She laughed.

He pointed out a large building with a flag hanging from an angled rod and a huge porch stretching across its front. "That's it, the VFW building, and the building next to it is the post office where my father worked for thirty-five years. And over here"—he took off across the street, pulling Brittany along with him—"is the store that gainfully employed me for . . . oh, forever, it seemed."

They were standing in front of a grocery store with a painted sign that read WASSINK'S GROCERIES in faded red letters.

Brittany peered through the dusty windows at wooden counters and tall shelves crammed full of packages and cans, and tried to imagine the man beside her as a young boy spending hours in this store. She couldn't. "Sam the Renaissance man, in an apron, slicing up bologna . . . I think I need time to adjust to all this."

He laughed and pulled her close, his hand moving up to rest on her shoulder.

"I delivered groceries sometimes, and clerked and soothed hurt feelings when Gus Wassink scolded girls for buying lipstick and boys for hanging around and reading his magazines and housewives for talking too softly."

"He was something of a character?"

"You might say so, but not a bad sort of fellow if you looked deep enough."

She studied Sam's face as he talked and listened for words that weren't spoken. His eyes were bright with memory, but they didn't tell her what she wanted to know: Had he had fun here? Had he joked and laughed and entertained, like he did with the folks at the Elms? Had he charmed the girls and had they hung around to flirt with him?

But he caught her hand again, wove his fingers through hers, and moved on. "The church is around the corner, and there's a local hospital that all the people here use, St. Francis Xavier. Both my brother and I were born there."

"Your brother?"

He nodded. "Baby brother Joseph. Joe Lawrence. He's a nice person and about as different from me as any mortal could be, which, I guess, is a blessing. He was perfectly content here and left only because he wanted to go to a teacher's college and Shadyside didn't have one."

"Did he come back?"

"No, but almost. He married a fellow teacher from a tiny little town in northern Pennsylvania and they live a replica of Shadyside life there."

"Were you and Joe buddies growing up?" She was listening intently to his answers, trying to sort through these new views of Sam, trying to see how they fit together. It was all a surprise to her, and she couldn't say why, but Shadyside and Sam seemed an uncomfortable match.

"Not buddies," he answered, "Not exactly." He once

again led her across the street and headed for a sign with HUGE HAMBURGERS outlined in neon lights. "Joe was several years younger and I was kind of responsible for him. That made being a buddy hard. Mom worked at a department store and I was the one around most. When I was working, I took Joey with me."

"He was pretty dependent on you, I guess."

"Yep. Which is why I stayed around here as long as I did." He glanced at Brittany. She was listening so carefully, but was she hearing what he was saying?

Her eyes grew larger and she squeezed his hand. "It must have been difficult as a teen, being responsible for someone else like that."

"Oh, you do what you do. And I would never have shirked it, not for a minute. I loved Joey. But having someone that dependent on me kept me here, and also taught me some important things about myself.

"God made certain people certain ways, and He must have given me an extra set of wings, because no matter what happened, I never felt comfortable here. It was claustrophobic. I was always looking for the rainbow, wanting to taste the rest of the world, to move on, to learn new things. I never resented Joey, but I knew I wasn't cut out to have someone dependent on me like that—forever. Sometimes, just because of the way I felt, I thought I was cheating Joey."

"So you finally got away," she said softly.

He nodded thoughtfully. "I don't mean it was the people here I was getting away from, Brittany. They were fine people. But no one understood, no one felt that same pull to explore and digest that world out there with the same intensity I did. And when I finally was able to move on, well, it was *wonderful*. Like a parched spirit finally finding water and nourishment. I went off to Penn State, a little late but no worse for wear, and the world opened up for me. Things I'd never touched before the way I wanted to—music and art and plays. Different kinds of people and philosophies.

And after college I plunged into every opportunity that came along. I guess I'm still catching up, moving on to each thing life has to offer."

"It seems to me you've done a pretty good job, Sam. You've experienced so many things."

He wove his fingers into her hair as they walked and considered her words. "There's a *lifetime* of different things out there, Brittany."

The smile in his eyes spread across his whole face, and Brittany found herself caught up in the magic of the moment. He was lost in a dream, flying away. Making sure his parents' kind of life didn't settle upon him and hold him fast.

"And speaking of tasting different things . . ." He stopped in the middle of the sidewalk, his eyes fixed on the garish neon sign. A crooked grin curved his lips. "We have here Jake's famous hamburgers, guaranteed to fill even a teenager's bottomless belly. What do you say, Brittany? Doesn't the smell alone lift your spirits?"

She looked at the cafe-curtained windows, then grinned up at Sam. "At this point, raw hot dogs would be welcome! Let's try it." She tugged on his hand and they pushed their way through the heavy glass door.

Settled in a shadowed booth and fortified with huge mugs of hot chocolate delivered by a short-skirted teenager, Brittany and Sam smiled tiredly at each other.

"What a day," she said. "My mind feels nicely full."

He leaned his head against the back of the booth and concentrated on the golden flecks that danced in her eyes. "Full of what?"

"Oh, thoughts of you mostly. And now I need to digest all this and see what I can make of it." Her light laughter only partially hid the jumble of emotions their afternoon together had stirred up. It would take a while to sort it all out. And for what purpose? She shook her head slowly and looked up into Sam's thoughtful eyes. "Maybe I ought to digest some food first."

He leaned forward, propping his elbows on the table,

and cupped both her hands between his. His head bent close enough for her to feel his breath and smell the autumn cold that clung to his jacket.

The smile was there, and the laughter and light flowing from his incredibly dark eyes. She swallowed around the lump in her throat and met his gaze.

"Brittany, don't think too hard about any of it. It's just background, like your having gone to Sarah Lawrence."

She nodded, smiling, but knowing just as surely as Sam did that the past *did* matter—and one's reaction to what had happened there mattered—and that it *was* worth thinking about. In sifting through the past, the present often became more clear. And sometimes even the future . . .

Platters were slid between them, and she sat back and stared at a burger large enough to feed six. "Sam!" She laughed, relieved to concentrate on something as easily analyzed as food. "How did you ever manage to keep in shape eating stuff like this?" She eyed the crisp hard roll and the butter dripping in yellow puddles along the plate and felt her stomach growl.

"Isn't it great?" He lifted a golden fried onion ring from the basket and held it up to her mouth, one finger crooked gently beneath her chin.

She took a tiny bite, looking over the onion ring at Sam. The faint stirring was back. And the rushing warmth in her arms and legs as well as other places she dared not think about right now. She swallowed the bite of onion.

He wiped a tiny crumb of batter from the corner of her mouth with his finger. Her lips were petal-soft and he could barely keep from tasting them right there in the middle of Jake's Burger Shop. His chest was tight and the only thing in the room that he could see with clarity were Brittany's lovely green eyes.

The heat in the small booth was enough to keep her warm for the whole winter, Brittany decided hazily.

She loved the feel of his finger on her lips, but she pulled his hand away, holding it between hers, so she could talk. "Thank you for bringing me here," she said huskily.

His laughter warmed her even more. "I don't quite know how it happened, how we ended up here, but it was a nice journey. I suppose everyone should visit Shadyside at least once."

She nodded solemnly. "Not to mention sampling a side of beef."

Sam glanced up at the clock behind her. Nearly seven-thirty. Where do they go from here? He and this lovely, flowering woman who was spinning a web clear around him. He couldn't leave her, that he felt in every part of himself. Not quite seven-thirty. Thursday evening. Thursday evening! He threw his head back and groaned painfully. "Oh, Brittany . . ."

"Sam!" Startled, she sat upright. "What is it?"

"*It* is Uncle Felix Winters."

She looked frantically around the empty shop. "Uncle Felix? Sam, what are you talking about?"

"I have an appointment tonight to talk to your uncle Felix about the game. I don't understand it. I don't usually forget appointments."

She let out a sigh of relief. "Sam, don't scare me like that. What time is your meeting?"

"Eight-thirty. At his men's club."

She slid out of the booth, her mind trying to collect and control the unleashed feelings still floating freely inside of her. A rush of disappointment washed through her. She'd wanted the day to go on and on and on. She didn't want to think rationally, she just wanted to *feel*, because the way Sam made her feel was delicious and sweet and she couldn't seem to get enough of it. Her eyes met his and she knew it flowed out easily, what she felt. It was plain and simple. She wanted the feeling to grow until it exploded. She wanted Sam to make love to her.

"Would he understand if I had a sudden case of yellow fever and rescheduled?" Sam's voice was husky.

She shook her head slowly. "No, Sam, not Uncle Felix. One *never* breaks an appointment with Uncle Felix." She tore her gaze from him and walked toward the door.

"Not even for emergencies?" He was right behind her and his breath was warm on her neck. "I don't think our day is over, Brittany . . . I'd like to spend more time with you."

Her hand was on the door and her heart was somewhere high up inside her, beating rapidly. She turned slowly and managed a smile that matched nothing she felt. "Sam, I was late once for a meeting with Uncle Felix . . . an appointment I had . . . to sell him girl scout cookies."

He slipped his hands into her hair and held her head back so he could see her face. "And . . . ?"

"And . . . he reported the tardiness to the National Council of Scouting . . . for my own good . . ."

Sam bent and kissed away the ending of her words, his lips blotting out all sound except heartbeats and the dim noise of traffic in the background. Finally he pulled away and looked up, just as the round clock down the street began to fill the air with ringing bongs. Small groups of men moved along the street, jacket collars lifted to ward off the night chill.

Brittany looked after them, then reached up and stroked his cheek. "Poker, Sam. It's not for us. Come, Uncle Felix is waiting."

Five

The next afternoon Brittany stood in front of a nondescript office door. She had taken the day off from Petpals, letting the volunteers chauffeur the pets around while she ran various necessary errands—like grocery shopping. Sam had said he'd be working on her father's game at his office, and had invited her to drop by. This was the first time she'd been to Sam's office and when no one answered her knock, she checked the address he'd scribbled on a piece of paper to make sure it was the right number. Suite 103. That's what he'd said, although he hadn't mentioned it was in an old brownstone in the renovated section of Windemere. The building had been carefully fixed up and quartered into offices. It was a pleasant surprise from the usual squat, concrete office building, *if* it was the right place. But there was nothing on the door that said Creative Games, nothing at all to indicate this was Sam's business. Just painted numbers on the smoked glass surface. Beyond the door she could hear music playing softly. A symphony . . . ? Puzzled, she knocked again, and this time the door opened a crack. She stepped through, and her eyes widened.

The outer office was crammed full of cardboard boxes,

one on top of the other in haphazard fashion. Some were still closed, while the contents of others—dice and brightly colored playing pieces—spilled out onto the clean floor. And nothing else. No furniture. No cheerful plants. No desk. No *living person.* But filling the air were the wonderful themes of a Brahms sonata that came from a rather elaborate stereo system lined up against one wall.

She shook her head and stuck her hands into the pockets of her wool slacks. Strange. Perhaps she should have called first. She enjoyed the music for a moment, then gave the room one more cursory glance and walked with growing curiosity into the next room.

There was hope here, she decided, though no life. Several desks were positioned about the room at odd angles and a drawing board stood in front of a window. Mugs filled with artists' tools were lined up neatly on the sill.

She walked over to the drawing board and glanced at the sheet of paper lying across the smooth surface.

"THE GORDON WINTERS GAME" was sketched in neat letters in the center of the white sheet and was bordered on all sides by game squares. The name of the New England town in which her father was born was printed in one, the church in which he'd been married in another, and so on around the board. Beneath the words tiny cartoon-type characters romped across the squares, acting out the events.

She smiled and her heart skipped a beat. This wasn't at all what she had anticipated when the game idea had been explained to her a little over a week ago. What Sam was undertaking was a thoughtful, gentle exploration; it wasn't a mechanical study at all. In fact, Sam's way of questioning her had been so subtle, she'd felt he was doing it because he cared about *her*, as a *person*, not as a client or a source or a reference. He was making it all as painless as eating candy.

She took a deep breath and walked through the final

door into what must have been a kitchen in the original house. A round butcher-block table was set in front of shuttered windows, and a tiny stove and refrigerator were still in place. One window was open to let in the crisp autumn breeze and through it Brittany heard animated voices. She stepped closer and looked out through the thin curtain.

Beyond the window and stretching the width of the brownstone was a tiny square patch of patio. An old picnic table stood beneath the one tree—a proud maple whose brilliantly colored leaves drifted down in slow motion to the uneven brick below. Leaning against the tree, his pipe held loosely in a hand that moved slowly through the air, was Sam Lawrence.

Brittany stopped short, her pulse quickening. A feeling of familiarity rushed through her so suddenly it startled her.

With two fingers she pulled the curtain back and let her gaze run freely over the shadowed figure beneath the tree. He wore jeans today, and a tan V-neck sweater over his shirt, and the same crooked smile that was laced through her dreams. His standing position afforded her a view that not only brought attention to the rugged lines of his face but emphasized the muscular strength of his beautifully proportioned body as well. Even in a casual stance he seemed brimming with carefully controlled energy, a kind of energy she wanted to touch with her fingers and feel with her body. She shivered, but continued to stare unabashedly, her gaze traveling slowly across the hard curve of his shoulders and the expanse of chest, then on downward until the catch of her own breath in her throat made her stop short.

She pinched her eyes shut and breathed deeply to quell the gushing warmth rising within her. Finally, feeling some semblance of control return, she looked out the window again and noticed the others for the first time.

Seated at the table were three people, all listening attentively to Sam, laughing comfortably at intervals, and scribbling occasionally on yellow legal pads.

All were in their early twenties, Brittany guessed, and were dressed as casually as Sam. The only female in the group was a dark-haired woman. Her hair was pulled loosely back into a French braid and she wore an attractive sweater and jeans. She was pretty, Brittany thought, concentrating on the girl's pleasant smile and shapely figure. She watched her ask Sam a question, then leaned closer to the window to assess his answering smile.

Even from a distance she could see it was a friendly, satisfied group. They smiled like people who shared jokes and knew each other well.

She spotted a back door next to the sink and walked quickly through it. Best not be caught spying.

"Brittany!" Sam spotted her immediately and his warm smile welcomed her out into the sunshine. "Wonderful! I was hoping you'd make it. Come meet the crew." He was at her side in three long strides and slid his arm around her waist. "This skeptical hodgepodge of humanity is claiming you're a figment of my overactive imagination."

"But I can see you are definitely quite real," broke in a bearded man. Sam introduced him as Gary Williams, the artist who created the game boards. Gary's eyes were admiring as he shook her hand. "So happy to meet the lovely muse who has Sam working so hard."

"Oh, to the contrary. Sam's the slave driver," she said, then turned to meet Tim Warner and Jill Ford, the two game designers who worked under Sam's direction.

Sam stayed close beside her, his fingers playing lightly on her waist. "We were ironing out some wrinkles in the game and hoped the weather would inspire us," he said. "But now we have *real* inspiration."

"It's going to be a top-notch game, Brittany," Jill said. "I think your father will be pleased."

"What a frontiersman your father was," Tim added with respect in his voice. "He wasn't afraid to try anything, was he?"

Brittany fought to concentrate on the designer's words. Sam's fingers had played their game along her waist, and now they'd dipped beneath the edge of her sweater and traveled slowly back and forth across the smooth bare skin of her back. "Yes," she murmured, "I guess he has broken his share of new ground. And I can see his life is in good hands here."

That, at least, was true enough. But when she looked sideways and caught the flashing light in Sam's eyes, she wondered fleetingly what was happening to her own careful life.

Sam's slow smile gave her no answer.

"Well, Brittany, what do you think of the crew?" Sam stashed his notes into a tan file holder, then turned his attention back to the woman sitting in an old leather chair near the window. He'd had trouble all afternoon keeping his eyes off her. Bless Uncle Felix! He'd kept Sam for hours last night, carefully detailing twenty years of Gordon Winters's life, and nearly as much of his own. And Sam had smiled and responded, and all the while had slowly, tenderly, made love to Brittany in his mind. Just the sight of her this afternoon had brought it all back, the tightness, the sensations—

"I like them, Sam," she said. "They're exhilarating. Ideas flew around here so fast, I felt as if I were in the middle of a Ping-Pong game."

He picked up his pipe and leaned against the edge of the desk. "Good, I thought you'd approve. They're great kids—and their differences mesh like a Monet painting."

"Where did you find them?" She tilted her head to one side and watched the smoke circle slowly above his head.

"Here and there. I asked around. Jill is fresh out of Harvard. Quick as a whip and has a creative bent that doesn't stop. She thought she'd go off to New York and find herself, but I corralled her with my charm and taught her about making games. And she's terrific at it."

"And Tim?"

"Tim was one of those kids who never fit in anywhere because no one understood the intricacies of his mind. The ideas that kid comes up with are incredible. I know he'll push Creative Games into whole new directions." Sam's face lit up with excitement as he spoke, the pipe moving in rhythm with his words, his eyes flashing. "It'll be something, you wait and see, Brittany Ellsbeth Winters. And you can say you were here in the early days." His husky laugh rumbled through the cluttered office.

"I don't doubt that in the slightest, Sam. In the few short days I've known you, I've become convinced you can do most anything you put your mind to."

"Well, maybe that's a *slight* exaggeration. Just a tad, though, mind you." He laughed, a comfortable, infectious laugh that easily pulled Brittany into it.

"What kind of plans *do* you have for Creative Games?" she asked.

"Well . . ." He took a thoughtful draw on his pipe and stared off into space. "What I'd really like to do is make sure it can stand on its own two legs with enough clients to hold it up and support the kids—"

"There you go again. Sam, they're not kids!"

He laughed. "Yeah, you're right. They're only kids when I remember that I started college when they were still running around and skinning their knees."

"How old are you?"

"Thirty-five, I think. Age has never had much bearing on what I do or don't do, though, so I don't ever pay much attention to it. Anyway, I'd like to see that Jill, Gary, and Tim are earning enough to make it worth their while. Then I'll turn it over to them and let them run with it."

Brittany brushed aside the feeling of uneasiness that swept over her. "You'd leave the company?"

"Oh, I can never let go of things completely. I'd hang around and on occasion push my nose into whatever they were doing. Let them tell me to get lost. 'Consult,' as the pros say. But I'd look for another project, mostly."

"Here in Windemere?"

Sam paused for just a moment before answering. He'd been in Windemere nearly eighteen months this time. That was a long time. Yet somehow the words didn't spill out as quickly as they usually did when he talked about moving on. Something about Brittany was tugging at him. Besides the physical pull—and that was as powerful as dynamite—there was something different, a feeling of being connected to her—or understanding, or something crazy. Lord knew he'd never ended up in Shadyside before when he'd had a beautiful woman sitting beside him in the car! No, Brittany was different. He gazed into her clear green eyes and tried to make things fall into place. But the feeling remained. He shook his head and answered slowly, "No, probably not in Windemere, Brittany."

"Where, then?" Her voice was low. She'd known him such a short time, yet the thought of him leaving was planting an inexplicable sadness in her. And it didn't make an ounce of rational sense.

He shrugged. "I don't ever make decisions far in advance. Things just kind of happen. When the time's right, I'll move on. There are a lot of things I'd like to do. Life's so short, Brittany. And I like to keep what there is of it full."

"But moving so often, pulling up roots . . ."

"There's not much problem there because I never put *down* roots. Like this office." His hand swept through the air. "It's very hard for me to think in terms of permanent, Brittany. Jill and Tim are always on my back to take time to settle in. I know I should—for their sake—but it doesn't come naturally and seems to always take a backseat to something more pressing."

Brittany pulled her thoughts together and concentrated on the cluttered room, a far easier target than the gnawing uncomfortableness of Sam's wanderlust. "It could use a little organizing, Sam, it really could. Just a few homey touches . . ." In her mind she was already arranging and painting and filling the shadowy corners with lush green plants. She was filled with an irrational, urgent need to make the small office a permanent-looking place. A place Sam would like. "It wouldn't take much, Sam. I could help." She threw him what she hoped was a carefree grin. She was up out of the chair now, walking through the door into the other room, then back again, seeing things that weren't there, but could be with little effort.

"Brittany, stop." He followed her around, laughing. "You've far more important things to do than make sense of this mess. Like eating dinner with me, for example. I'm starving."

But Brittany wasn't listening. All her energy was directed on these three rooms. She'd discovered a wonderful cache of shelves hidden behind folding louvered doors in one room and was busy shoving boxes toward their future home.

"Here, Sam." She handed him a letter opener. "Open these boxes and empty everything onto the shelves." She glanced down at her watch. "Do you have a phone?"

He pointed toward the other room. "On the box near the window."

She grinned and disappeared.

Sam bent down beside a box and puffed quietly on his pipe lost in thought of Brittany Winters. She wasn't easy to anticipate or second-guess. But he liked that, among a *whole* lot of other things.

She was back in minutes, cheeks glowing and energy radiating about her. "Sam, at the rate you're moving, we'll be here till Christmas. Here." She knelt down beside him, her shoulder rubbing his side as she scooped out bags of playing pieces. "These go on the bottom shelf."

He felt her body heat against his arm and inhaled the clean sweet smell of her fully and deliberately. In her soft wool slacks and that patterned sweater that emphasized the full curve of her breasts, she was all the decoration any office could possibly need. But she wouldn't believe that, he decided, nor could he convince her to stay in that spot forever, so he took the plastic bags from her and smiled. "Yes, boss."

Her slim body moved in rhythmic motions back and forth across the room, up and down, dipping into boxes and thrusting the contents into his hands. "Sam," she said quietly, her eyes intent on the boxes she was shoving into the hallway with the toe of her shoe, "how do you see the rest of your life?"

He looked up, surprised. "The rest of my life?"

She nodded and walked back into the room. "Do you see it as a series of moves from one thing to another as you wander across the world? Or is there a pot of gold somewhere that will lure you to settle down? Or—"

"Whoa! Those are a lot of soul-searching questions you've spilled out, my love."

"Seriously, Sam." She turned and threw some scraps of packing material into a trash bag. "I'm just curious. Is there something at the end of all this? Or does an end simply mean you find another beginning?"

He let the box he was lifting slide back down to the floor and picked his pipe up out of the ashtray. Every damn one of her questions was legitimate. But no one had ever asked him those things before and he'd never tried to put together answers. "I honestly can't say, Brittany." His voice was thoughtful. "I guess I don't really think about life that way, so linear, with a beginning and end."

"It's chapters, then? Like in a book?"

"Maybe more like that, yes. Or maybe a book of short stories." He watched her move some pictures and thought about what he had just said. It didn't sound right. A book of short stories meant different characters in each. Then Brittany would be in only one, and he was slowly coming to think he couldn't bear that. He shook his head. "No, erase that book of short stories. I need to think more about this one, Brittany. You're taxing the old mind."

She laughed uneasily and handed him a box to look through. "Maybe I'm being presumptuous, Sam, or too nosy. . . ."

"No, not that." It wasn't that at all. Brittany could ask him his soul's secrets if she wanted to. But he couldn't pursue the conversation any further right now for other reasons. Mostly because he hadn't the faintest idea what the answers were anymore.

"Okay, Sam. You need to go through these." She handed him a stack of loose papers and remained standing, looking down on him while he went through the stack, throwing some out and saving others. "See, Sam? You, too, can sort and trash."

His long legs were stretched out in front of him now, his back flat against a filing cabinet. "Only with a benevolent dictator beside me." He caught her hand and drew her down beside him."Hmmm, there's a glow about you, Brittany."

"That's dust, Sam."

"Then it's fairy dust, because it's doing things to me."

"Do you have to sneeze?" she teased, aware of the slow heat building between them. She unfolded her legs and stretched them out, too, one of her legs lined up alongside his body, their hips touching lightly.

"No, I don't think I have to sneeze," he said. "Although what I'm feeling is similar."

She laughed a little self-consciously. His voice had grown unusually husky.

"Interesting." She busied her hands stacking the papers he'd scattered across her knees and wrinkled her forehead in thought. "It's caused by fairy dust . . . and makes you feel something like sneezing. . . . Hiccups, maybe?"

"Hiccups aren't caused by fairy dust, Brittany. Everyone knows that."

"Silly of me," she said weakly. She stared at his shadowed chin, then bravely lifted her eyes to gaze into the gleaming depth of his. They spoke even more eloquently than his voice, which was echoing inside her. Does memory capture voices? she wondered fleetingly. "I heard about a lady who made a sculpture out of dust once. Is that what it makes you want to do?"

He shook his head. "It was lint, I think, that she used." His hand slipped beneath the papers and massaged her thigh.

"Similar," she said just as the stereo filled the room with the sounds of Beethoven's Fifth Symphony. A deep rumbling hum from Sam's throat echoed the staccatoed sound of the violins.

She felt the sound deep in her bones and delighted in it. "A classical hummer . . ." She raised her face to his and smiled, unafraid.

"I've been called worse," he murmured as he lifted one hand and caressed her cheek. "Brittany . . ."

"I know," she managed to whisper above the hammering of her heart. "It wasn't a sneeze you felt at all."

He leaned forward so he could look directly into her face. Her green eyes were shining and the soft tangle of her hair framed her flushed cheeks. He curled one hand around her neck and held her head gently. "Oh, Brittany, you are without a doubt the most beautiful creature I've ever known." His breath caught in his throat and for a split-second Sam Lawrence felt a totally new, totally alien sensation rush through his body: the stinging wonder of tears. His slow smiled pushed the feeling away, but he'd remember it later, the power Brittany had to move him in unexpected ways.

Searching his coffee-colored eyes, Brittany watched the play of his emotions. His eyes almost seemed to change color, then deepen in intensity until she felt mesmerized. "Sam . . ."

His fingers delved into her silky hair and he bit back a groan. She felt so *real* to him, so incredibly soft and perfect. Desire flared in his loins and he stiffened, fighting for control. "What, Brittany?"

"Are you . . . habit-forming?"

She shifted slightly when she spoke and her breasts rubbed lightly against his chest. "Oh, I hope so, sweet Brittany, I certainly hope so." He closed the minuscule space between them until the feel of her smooth, pliant lips pushed talk and reason beyond his reach. Lord, he wanted her so badly he could feel it in every crevice, every nerve ending and tiny patch of skin. His kiss deepened with the force of his emotion and his tongue gently circled inside her mouth, dipping and tasting.

Brittany closed her eyes and let her whole body relinquish itself to the pleasure of his kiss. She wanted it to go on at least forever, an endless joining. The depth of her breathing pushed her breasts tight against him and she felt her nipples grow firm and hard.

"Hmmm," he murmured into the heated space between their lips. "You fit just right." His fingers slipped from beneath her hair and lightly grazed her cheek, then moved down until he rubbed gently against her breast.

Pleasure pounded through her, blurring the late afternoon sunshine filtering through the windows and the lovely strains of Beethoven still filling the quiet room. Only Sam's touch and smell and the wonderful feel of his body was real.

"Ahem!"

Brittany heard the noise somewhere off in the distance, somewhere behind her. It was a disconnected noise, intruding into the moment.

"Anyone home?"

Sam reluctantly pulled himself away and looked over her shoulder to the open doorway.

She sat still and forced the dreamy fog away with deep breaths of cool air.

"It's a jolly green giant," Sam said softly into her ear, a slow smile crossing his face.

She half-turned, her body still enticingly close to his, and followed his gaze.

Two blue-jeaned legs stuck out from beneath a huge ficus tree. Between the branches the freckled face of a young man peeked out.

"Knock knock."

"Clyde!"

"Hi, Miss Winters. How're things?" The plant was dropped to the floor unceremoniously, revealing a skinny, grinning teenager.

"You two have met?" Sam pulled himself up from the floor and looked from Brittany to the fellow sticking his hands into the pockets of his worn jeans.

"Yeah, I know Miss Winters real good. Since forever."

"Clyde . . ." Brittany began. Her hands went to her cheeks in an attempt to nonchalantly cool away the heated blush. "Clyde Johnson from Johnson's Greenhouse, Sam. Hello, Clyde." She reached for Sam's hand and pulled herself up beside him.

Clyde looked down at the floor. "Sorry I'm late, Miss Winters. Couldn't get the truck started." He looked back up and grinned at Sam. "It's twenty-one years old. A Ford. Can you believe she still runs?"

Sam shook his head obligingly. "Amazing."

"And it holds a forest, pretty near. Come here and see."

Sam followed Clyde to the door and looked down the hallway. Two more ficus trees leaned against the wall, along with several hanging ivies, a schefflera, and a few potted flowering plants.

"Well, Clyde," Sam said, "you seem to be right about

the forest." His thoughts circled back to Brittany and how perfectly she had fit in his arms.

Brittany glanced beyond the two men, and when she did, her head seemed to clear. "These are just fine, Clyde. Really nice. Let's bring them on in."

"The forest is coming in?" Sam asked slowly, forcing his attention back to the mounds of living greenery just outside his doorway.

Brittany turned smiling eyes toward him. "Yes, Sam. Besides being good for the air, these plants will be just the right touch for your office. Trust me." She lightly fingered a leaf on the ficus tree and rubbed off a spot of dust, then lifted the tree and carried it over to a window.

Good for the air? Sam repeated silently. What he needed now was something good for calming the fires Brittany Winters had lit within him. Plants somehow didn't seem to be the answer. "But I didn't—"

"No. I called before and arranged it with Mr. Johnson. And Clyde was happy to bring them over. Don't say a word, Sam, until you see how they look." The air was finally cooling and Brittany felt her voice leveling off.

"But—"

"I'll show Jill or Gary how to take care of them. You won't have to worry about a thing."

"They must have cost a fortune."

Clyde shook his head vigorously. "We have a deal with Miss Winters, sir. No problem. She takes good care of my grandpop out at the Elms, y'know." He added as an afterthought, "And we take 'em back if they die or you leave town or something."

Sam was put in charge of carting boxes out to the dumpster behind the building and moving desks into pleasing positions. He tried to capture Brittany as she glided from room to room, tried to suggest Clyde leave and they finish their decorating in better light—like tomorrow's sunlight.

But Clyde refused to budge as long as Brittany might

need him, and Brittany seemed again caught up in beautifying his office.

"Brittany, this can wait. . . ." He caught her for a brief moment, his palm gently cupping her chin.

But she ducked away from his touch and swept at the desktop. "Almost done, Sam." When she was in his arms, she lost all reason. All she wanted was to press herself to him, to feel his body against hers, giving it life. But an affair was the last thing in the world she wanted in her life. Not with a man who would sail off into the sunset when it was over. Damn! She wanted him . . . she didn't want him. . . . Decorating was certainly far easier to deal with! She jerked a plant from the floor and flew across the room.

"Now?" Sam asked a half hour later after he finally managed to usher Clyde back to his truck.

Brittany looked around. She'd found a few soft, comfortable chairs in the basement, some brass lamps Sam had forgotten he had, and together with the plants, the home of Creative Games looked beautiful. The outer office even had a scattering of magazines on an old oak coffee table, and she had hung several game boards along one wall in a way that suggested the place had real class.

"I can't believe it," Sam whispered in her ear. "You're amazing, Miss Winters."

She smiled, pleased at his praise. "Thank you, sir. The open-box look was nice, but I think the crew will like this too."

"'They'll think I've gone off the deep end."

He leaned closer, and his warm breath on her neck made her shiver. Her heart began its familiar racing and she felt the heat of tiny embers that would burst into flame any second. She couldn't even trust herself anymore! Wrapping her arms tightly around her waist, she nibbled on her bottom lip and stared into the distance to try to consider Sam Lawrence objectively.

But his long hands rubbing up and down her arms

made objectivity quite difficult. She caught his fingers and tried to stop the slow, sensuous movement.

He slowly turned her around until she faced him. "You've made a big difference here, Brittany."

"Thank you, Sam," she managed to say as she concentrated on calming her heartbeat. "And now for my payment . . ."

"You name it, Brittany." His voice had thickened, and she could hardly trust her own.

"Promise me . . . that the plants will be watered. . . ."

She seemed so vulnerable as she stood there, he thought, her face turned up to his. This strong, mothering woman who helped old people face the end of their lives with joy . . . He wanted to scoop her up, to protect her, to let her know it would be okay. That joy was okay. And loving. That they could handle it all, and it would be all right, because he'd never hurt her. No matter what it took, he wouldn't do that. But beneath his hands he could feel her little quivers of fear.

He brushed a silken lock of hair off her forehead and smiled. "Sure, Brittany. I'll be sure the plants are taken care of. But now I'd like to take care of *you*, if I may. Dinner, at least?"

She hesitated for a fraction of a second, not daring to look into his eyes. She knew the force she would see there would be beyond anything she could handle tonight. She knew she wanted Sam Lawrence desperately. She wanted to love him and to have him love her. She wanted to feel his hands on her breasts and his lips on her body. She wanted to see him naked, to slide her lips over his skin and trace his muscles with her fingers, and run her hands down the whole lovely length of him.

So many *wants*, so many deafening desires. She could barely hear herself when she looked up into his bottomless brown eyes and spoke calmly and carefully.

"Sorry, Sam. I have a family dinner tonight. It's Sara's birthday."

His face was filled with a look of such boyish disappointment that it softened the painful edge of her budding passion, and she nearly took him into her arms to comfort him. Nearly, but not quite. It wasn't the time to slip back into the quicksand. . . .

"You're not going to let me thank you?"

When he smiled like that, the boyishness was swallowed up quickly in the sensuous curve of his lips, and she shifted her concentration to the slight cleft in his chin. "No thank-yous necessary, Sam."

Sam noticed her eyes were focused on his chin and he began rubbing it. "Plant dirt? Mind wiping it off for me?"

She lifted her gaze to his laughing eyes. "You're quite impossible, Sam. But I'm strong." She pulled back her shoulders comically and sucked in a giant lungful of air. "See? I can weather tornadoes, even ones that walk and talk and sometimes take my breath away."

He lifted his hand to her cheek and stroked it tenderly.

The warmth seeped all the way through her. She closed her eyes briefly and let it settle in the very center of her. When she opened them again, there was a new look shining from his own eyes, a gentle, caring look that was almost as difficult to handle as the smoldering passion she'd seen earlier.

"I'd better go, Sam."

He nodded, and placed a soft, tender kiss on her lips before dropping his hand. "Good night. And give Sara my best birthday wishes."

She nodded and walked over to the door, then stopped and looked back. "Are you staying here?"

He shook his head. There was plenty of work to do, but he'd get nothing done tonight, not with the sweet smell of her lingering in the air. "I'm going to find someplace to eat. And, since there will be no one around to offend, I think I'll find the hottest, most garlicky chili in town, pile it with onions and peppers, and have a feast. Maybe that'll keep me warm."

She laughed and pulled open the door. "The least I can do is suggest the best. Try Hombres on North Henderson Street. They have chili that will make your ears smoke and eyes water for days. I guarantee it'll keep you warm. Sam."

His eyes brightened and his voice was laced with husky innuendo. "You'll guarantee it? There's only one thing I could guarantee would keep me warm . . ."

"Good night, Sam. Sweet dreams." She hurried out into the safe aloneness of the night.

Six

"Are you asleep?"

Brittany shook her head sleepily into the pillow and attempted to open her eyes, but the task was too great. Rolling over, she slid comfortably back into a wonderful dream.

"Brittany?"

She nodded again, smiling, her head moving in slow motion. Only then did she realize she was nodding to a telephone receiver hanging loosely from one hand.

"Are you awake?" The rumbling voice coming from the phone slowly broke into her dream and pushed it farther and farther away until finally she couldn't see it anymore.

"Awake?" she mumbled, her eyes still closed beneath the weight of sleep. "That's a . . . a rather foolish question . . . if . . . you think about it for any length of time."

"Hmmm, perhaps you're right." Sam's voice was deep and very wide-awake.

"Sam, what time is it?" She pried her eyes open and attempted to look out the window. A velvet, star-studded sky filled the opening.

"Let me see . . ."

"It's somewhere between the middle of the night and dawn. Am I close?"

"Well, you might say so. Actually that's rather a good guess for someone who sounds as sleepy as you do."

"It's a nasty habit. Sam. Believe it or not, I almost always sleep away these hours."

"Pity."

She pulled the comforter up to her chin and shivered. "You, I might guess, don't?"

"It depends. Two things for sure could keep me up." He held the phone close and felt her smile on the other end. "The first is the sky. It's a perfect sky tonight, Brittany. The wintry air is moving in and cleaning up all the stuff up there, making it so pretty to look at."

"Oh, Sam . . . you woke me up for a weather report?"

He ignored her remark. "The Seven Sisters winked at me, the Bear was growling in splendor. It was very special. I wish you'd been there to see it with me, Brittany."

She smiled. Dreamy images of standing on a mountaintop with Sam at her side, the star-filled sky a backdrop behind them, floated in front of her. "Sam, am I dreaming this?"

"I hope so. I hope you're dreaming about the two of us lost in a galaxy together, exploring the Milky Way, riding a comet—because the second thing that could keep me up till drawn breaks is being with you, Brittany."

"Sam," she said slowly. "Sam, have you been . . . drinking?"

His husky laughter swept away the icy night chill and teased another smile onto her lips.

"My darling Brittany, I've had only one beer, the one I used to wash down that hell-raising chili you kindly suggested I have this evening—"

"*Last* evening," she corrected him. "And Hombres has the finest chili in Maine."

"Ah, now I know you're waking up, to make such a

distinction in time and offer a food critique on top of it."

"Sam?"

"Yes, Brittany?"

"Why did you call me in the middle of the night?"

"Why did I call you? Well . . ."

She stirred beneath the downy quilt. She could imagine how his chocolate-colored eyes would look as they grew thoughtful, and how the laugh lines at the corners of his mouth would deepen.

"Well, Brittany, let me count the ways. . . ."

"Sam, take me seriously."

"Brittany, I'll take you any way you want."

Her heart lurched.

"I called you without thinking, Brittany," he went on, his voice quiet as he pushed ideas around in his head. "I just came in from looking at the heavens, and everywhere I looked, on every star, I saw you. Sometimes that means something, so I called to be sure you were all right. I . . . ah, seem to have take on something here I didn't count on."

'What—what do you mean, Sam?"

"I mean you, my dear Brittany. I like being with you, very much, and I find you creep into my thoughts at the damnedest times. And if you can do that to me, well, then somehow it seemed I could call you."

"I see. . . ."

"So that's why." He wondered what she looked like, touched by sleep, in that wonderful old brass bed that he'd seen through her bedroom door when he'd left her carriage house. Would she be stretched out, or curved into a warm ball? Her hair would be sexily mussed, her eyes hazy and flecked with moonlight. She probably wore a long flannel nightgown that wrapped itself around her and covered her feet from the cold, the kind that would slide with feathery softness up her legs and over her thighs and the gentle curve of her hips. Her cheeks would be flushed, her lips soft and gently parted.

"Well, Sam," she finally said, and he could hear her shallow, quick breathing, "I guess that's fair. Tell me . . . about the sky you saw."

He leaned his head back against the couch in his small den and kicked off his shoes. His lazy smile spilled over into his voice. "It was a wonderful sky, Brittany."

She gave in to the lovely cadences of his voice, sinking back into the plump pillows, closing her eyes and playing his words across the screen of her mind until they formed into images.

"The lights in the city blinked off about the time you went to sleep, leaving the galaxy shining in all its glory. Ursa Major was so low, I nearly reached up and touched her! And there are rich fields of stars everywhere tonight." His voice grew husky. "It's truly beautiful, the kind of thing you share with someone special."

"And the Milky Way?" she asked dreamily. "Tell me about the Milky Way, Sam."

"It's splashed so beautifully across the sky, you'd be sure you could walk along it to the other side."

She saw it clearly, two figures side by side, floating across the ebony sky on a glittering white carpet.

"I would have ventured across if you had been with me," he said.

"And what would we have found on the other side?" she asked. Night had soothed her fears and Sam's physical absence from the room left her feeling brave and daring. None of this was real anyway, it was all an enchanting dream. "Would we have found Oz, Sam?"

"Oz would have been just the beginning, my love. There would have been wonderland and paradise and fantasyland all wrapped up together."

"Mmm. Sounds nice. As nice a dream as a person could have." She burrowed deeper into the warmth of the covers and played with his words. Sam's presence was so real there beside her, she felt she could reach out and rub her hands across his chest.

They were both silent for a long moment, the phone line between them connecting their spirits as they frolicked as freely as children on a finely spun dream.

"Sam . . . ?" Her word sought him softly.

"Hmmm?"

"Are you falling asleep?"

"Asleep? If that means the nice, gently drugged feeling of having a beautiful woman beside me, then maybe I am."

"You seem close, Sam." She felt a gentle stirring within her.

"It's a strange thing, Brittany. I can feel you here, nestled right into my side with your hair rubbing against my cheek. It's very nice."

"We're a little crazy, Sam. It must have been the chili and the birthday cake." The stirring grew without warning into a dancing fire.

"I guess we'd better go to sleep." His voice was strangely thick.

"Yes. I guess we'd better." She licked her bottom lip and wondered how firm the Milky Way was.

"Brittany?"

"Yes?"

"Look out your window. And that will be my good night."

She didn't hear the click but knew Sam had hung up. She couldn't feel him there beside her anymore. Slowly she turned and looked out the window.

The blackness was pushed back and the stars had disappeared. Brilliant rosy streaks were moving up from the horizon and painting the sky with color, heralding the new dawn.

Seven

"I'm exhausted, Sam," Brittany said. "Absolutely wrung out. Why is that? A day with Petpals never used to tire me out this way." She lifted one brow and eyed him across the small wooden table in Ralph's Bar and Grill. The warmth of the fire in the rough stone fireplace in the corner was slowly seeping into her bones.

Sam's eyes were dark in the shadowy booth. He lifted one shoulder in a shrug. "Darned if I know, Brittany. "I'm not tired at all."

"It's you, Sam. You've cast my life into confusion."

"Don't let a little tea dance throw you."

She couldn't help but smile as she recalled the rather unorthodox entertainment he had helped engineer at the Elms today. Actually, he said it had been all Frances's idea. She had been complaining that the Elms needed some more lively activities, something other than bingo, and she and Sam had decided to start a play-reading group. But their first meeting, today, had been a dance in the physical therapy room.

Brittany's smile deepened as she remembered Sam gliding across the floor with Frances, then she shook her head. "It's not the tea dance that's thrown me, Sam, and you know it. It's you."

He captured her hand between both of his and rubbed it gently, noticing how long and slender her fingers were. Like a piano player's, he thought. Beautiful hands. There was so much about her he had yet to discover. Patiently he waited for her to say more.

"This working relationship isn't quite orthodox."

"Listen, Brittany, who's to say how people should work?"

"But half the time we don't even talk about the game, Sam. Today, for example—"

"Today, lovely lady, while enjoying a Strauss waltz with the director, I found out that your father has given money to build a gazebo and an exercise pool for the Elms, and that he used to go to school with the receptionist, and that once in grammar school he organized a picket line when he thought the school policy on homework was unfair to the kids."

Brittany's brows shot up. "I knew about the Elms, but a picket line . . . ?" A small, incredulous smile lifted the corners of her lips.

"*And* I breakfasted with Meredith O'Leary before you were probably out of your wonderful brass bed. She's the lady who handled your father's campaign when he ran as a Democratic candidate in an all-Republican district for city councilman, again because he thought things needed a little shaping up."

"And he lost."

"Doesn't matter. He should have won but the odds were against him. He knew he'd lose, but he'd wanted to make a point."

She nodded. "I don't know why Dad took risks like that. . . ."

"Kept him alive, Brittany." Sam rubbed her cheek with the back of his hand. "Meredith had dozens of stories to tell. Great stories. You know, I have yet to meet him, but in a funny sort of way I'm going to *miss* him when this is over."

And she was going to miss Sam Lawrence, she thought, in a not so funny sort of way.

"So, Brittany," he said softly, "I *am* working on the game when I'm with you."

"But I don't need to be there for you to do those things."

"That's where you're dead wrong. Having you by my side not only opens the doors to me—those people at the Elms *love* you, you know—but it's more than that. You have a spirit about you that conditions all this, heads me in the right direction. It's hard to explain. You *are* my lovely muse."

She studied him in the shadowed light, his handsome head bent as he spoke. When he lifted his head, the look in his eyes reached clear within her. "Is it upsetting you, Brittany?"

"No," she said too quickly. "I mean, not really. It's not working with you that's a problem, Sam."

"Good."

"It's simply you."

He raised one brow but kept silent.

"It's you and me."

"That's better."

"Sam, listen." She squeezed his fingers tightly.

"Okay. It's you and me and the fact that we seem to be liking each other *better than expected*."

His dramatic tone drew a smile from her.

"You might put it that way," she said.

"Or"—he ran a finger over the curve of her cheek, then slowly drew it across her lips—"one might say there is a kind of magnetism between us. An animal magnetism. A sexual magnetism." He paused. "Couldn't one?"

His charm wound around her until she leaned forward across the tabletop. "Yes, Sam, one could say that. One could also say that we're a—a *distraction* to each other."

He mulled that over while he played with her fingers.

"It's true, Sam. And you . . . well, I know you can't be getting much more sleep than I am after we talk on the phone before dawn every morning."

"Less."

"Well, there, you see? That can't be good for work—your work, or mine. And—"

He lifted her hand again and pressed her fingertips to his lips. His eyes were shining. She slipped her hand free and held it in her lap.

"And where will it go from here?" he asked. "Is that what's bothering you?"

She lowered her head and traced a wavy line across the tabletop with one finger. She nodded slowly. "Perhaps that sounds foolish to someone like you. But, Sam, I'm different in that way. I—"

"It doesn't sound foolish at all, Brittany," he said gently. "And it's that 'differentness' that's thrown me to the end of the universe here too."

She met his eyes. She wasn't very good at baring her soul like this, but she had started it. She might as well plunge in all the way. "The casual part of you and me disappeared a while back, and what's left is a problem."

He nodded. Lord, she was doing it again, he thought, drawing him into her with her eyes, throwing him off balance, out of touch with tomorrow. He wanted her so badly, his skin ached.

"And," she added so softly he could hardly hear her, "I'm not sure what to do about it. I think I need a little distance here."

"People make problems. I want you very badly, Brittany. That's not a problem, it's a pure, overwhelming desire that's driving me crazy."

She snagged a breath. "I know what you mean. Maybe it's all just physical, Sam . . ."

The words were hollow when they hit the air, and they laughed together. "It sure as hell is physical," Sam said. "I'll grant you that. I think the 'just' has some problems."

She nodded and looked down at the table again for an answer that wasn't there.

Sam cupped her face gently between his hands. "Brittany. I'm not saying it's not complicated. I'm not used to what's going on inside me, either, but I know one thing—it's not the kind of thing one throws away, problem or not."

No, she didn't want it to go away either. Maybe *that* was the problem. . . .

"Could we maybe settle into the feeling—whatever it means—for now?" he asked. "See what happens?"

His eyes did her in. They were so deep and searching, and she found she lost the strength to look away. But when she didn't look away, she felt herself sinking into a realm that wasn't safe. Was it all just a matter of time? A matter of time before the tide of emotion swept them up in the passion they both felt? A matter of time before it ended?

Sam's eyes told her he cared for her deeply. But what they didn't tell her was how he handled deep feelings. Did they turn to love? And if that, heaven forbid, was happening, how did a man sworn from permanent relationships handle love?

She forced a smile and tried unsuccessfully to quell the mixed messages traveling up to her brain. She'd been unable to read them correctly for days now. Why should this moment be different? "You've done peculiar things to my powers of judgment, Sam. I think I need a cup of coffee."

"No champagne? I think it's a rather auspicious occasion. I can say in absolute honesty, I've never before discussed calmly across a table what you and I are discussing."

"Which is . . . ?"

He tugged on a lock of her hair. "Whether or not we should give in to this incredible, passionate force that is pulling us together."

"I haven't ever discussed it before either," she said in a small voice.

Sam stroked her hair, not sure whether to laugh or wrap her tightly in his arms and carry her off with him. Instead, he leaned over and planted a gentle kiss on her lips, then pulled back slightly and whispered, "You're something else, Brittany Ellsbeth. And there's not another one like you, not a single star in the universe—and that deserves a toast."

She smiled back and tilted her head to one side. "Coffee will be fine, Sam. It will keep me awake just long enough to drive my van home and fall into bed." She brushed her hair back from her flushed face.

Sam flagged down a young waitress and charmed her into producing two cups of coffee instantly. "I guess we could both use some coffee," he said. "And sleep."

She cupped her hands around the hot mug and nodded. "Definitely sleep. I may even unplug the phone. Just in case, you know."

"Right, you never know when one of those wrong numbers is going to keep you up all night."

She smiled. "Or even a right number."

"Sometimes they're the worst kind," he said solemnly though there was laughter in his eyes. He pulled out a pencil and began drawing on a paper napkin.

"What are you doing?" she asked.

"Doodling."

"Oh." She looked closer. "That's my name."

"Brittany Ellsbeth Winters. Right. You're very astute, tired as you are."

She peered closer, but it was hard to see in the dim, smoky light. Finally she plucked the napkin up from the table and looked at it closely. "A game? You've sketched a game here, Sam. With my name on it!"

"Just imagine what the game cards would be."

"Sam, don't be silly."

"Girl charms fella. Collect five smackers from bank.

And, *Girl seduces fella over phone lines. Pass Go and collect a bundle."*

She was laughing now, the throaty sound filling the small booth. *"Boy's mind goes amuck; girl drives home and goes to bed."* She leaned across the table and kissed him gently on the forehead.

His shoulders sagged. *"Despondent boy wanders off into oblivion. Miss turn and seek help for heartache."* He looked up as she slipped out of the booth, then followed quickly. "You're sure you don't want to finish the game?"

She pushed her arms into her heavy jacket and shook her head. Her lips were smiling but a soft cloud covered her eyes. "I always lose at games, Sam. 'Night."

He shielded her against the cold breeze that assaulted them when they left the restaurant and walked her to the old van.

Then he went home and fell across his comfortable bed that usually crooned him to sleep in seconds.

But Brittany's words lingered in his mind like a heavy fog, and for yet another night sleep was long in coming.

"Well, Sam," Katherine Winters said gently into the phone, "she didn't say *why* she was leaving for the weekend, actually. But she did say she'd be back tomorrow evening."

"I see." Sam leaned back in his swivel chair, his gaze resting on the lush ficus plant near the window. What he saw instead was the tiny flicker of fear that had sparked in Brittany's eyes the night before. She'd never once, all day or evening, mentioned being gone for the weekend. An uncomfortable, restless feeling ate away at him.

"Is it urgent you reach her, Sam?" Katherine asked.

"Well, we have some things ready to go to the printer, and I needed to check them with her first." It could wait, he thought, but he couldn't. The urgency to see her was building in him like a bonfire. "Could I call her, Mrs. Winters?"

"That's a trifle difficult. You see, Gordon used the cottage as a getaway, and he never installed a telephone."

"How far away is this place, Mrs. Winters?"

"Oh, it's not too far," she answered quickly, as if the same thought had hit her at precisely the same moment. "Only a couple of hours the way my Gordon drives. You might be able to make it up and back before nightfall, Sam. I think that's a wonderful idea! Besides, Brittany sounded as if she could use a friend."

But not this one, he thought. Simple intuition told him Brittany had purposely put distance between the two of them, and he wasn't quite sure why. Hadn't they made some honest headway last night? She seemed almost afraid of him at times. Yet the astounding chemistry between them was undeniable. And he knew she felt it as powerfully as he did. It had been obvious in her kisses, and in her incredible gold-flecked eyes, and in her touch.

Suddenly, seeing her was the only option open.

"Maybe if I could do that," he said, "and just get her okay on this copy."

"Yes, dear. A very fine idea. Now, here are the directions."

Brittany pulled off the heavy hiking boots and knocked them hard against the back porch railing. Mud and matted leaves fell to the ground below. "That's just what we needed, Dunkin," she said aloud.

Dunkin's tail thudded happily against the wooden floor.

She chuckled. "Oh, you'd agree with anything, wouldn't you? But it *is* what we needed. We both look better." Her gaze shifted from the dog to the woods and the winding path she'd just come from.

She'd walked all the way down to the lake's edge and back, and the crisp breeze and damp air had performed its magic just as it always did, cleaning out the cobwebs, pulling the threads of her life closer together. Maybe she should just move up here permanently, she thought with a half smile. She could walk, and think, and feed the birds. Brittany the recluse.

She slipped out of her coat, hung it on the oak rack just inside the back door, and walked through the hall into the warm, spacious living room.

Although the family called it a cabin, the house on the edge of the woods was nearly the size of a small inn, with tastefully decorated bedroom suites on the second floor, an enormous stone fireplace in the living room, and a roomy kitchen with a polished pine floor and every modern convenience. From her earliest moments of memory, this had been her favorite place on earth. It was warm, peaceful, and secure.

She turned on the stereo. The soft strains of a classical guitar piece filtered into the room, and she curled up on the oversized leather couch. She closed her eyes, seeping herself in the piny smells of the room and the comfort of childhood memories. She'd had little sleep the night before, but just being up here, comforted by the wind whistling through the massive pine trees outside, calmed her body into restfulness. She'd make a fire, she mused sleepily. In just another minute . . .

Sam's knock an hour later went unheard.

He stepped back off the porch and walked around to the side of the house. There was no mistaking the Petpals van parked beside a clump of stately pine trees on the circular drive. Brittany was here—somewhere. The simple thought of seeing her washed away his tiredness from being lost on the narrow backroads of the Maine hills for the last couple of hours, and he smiled as he pulled his pipe from the pocket of his thick parka.

What a great place this was! He breathed in the fresh

air and stretched his stiff arms, rotating the fatigue out of his shoulders. He'd tried to imagine the cabin on the way up, the kind of place that would draw Brittany to it when her soul needed soothing. Next to coming to him, he couldn't imagine a better place for her to go. He again walked up the wide porch steps to the front door.

He should have brought his camera, he thought. This was one of those tiny spots on earth worth recording. The tall pines protecting the house seemed to bend in agreement as the wind bowed their slender tops. He watched the slow motion for a moment longer, then knocked once more on the door. When there was still no answer, he turned the knob, opened the door, and stepped inside.

She was curled up at one end of a large couch. The only sound in the room was the soft music that mixed sweetly with the wind outside, and Brittany's gentle breathing while she slept. He slipped out of his jacket and sat down on the other end of the couch, not for a moment taking his eyes off her.

It must be a nice dream, he mused, noticing the peaceful lines of her face.

Her soft flannel shirt had ridden up her body, exposing a V of pale, creamy skin just above the waistband of her jeans. Her legs were bent, and her stockinged feet barely touched his knees. But he felt them just the same, like a soft, pillowy caress. She moved once, and one foot slipped up onto his thigh and stayed there, light and still. He leaned back and drew gently on his pipe. He felt he could sit there forever, the soft leather of the couch supporting his body, and the wonderful feel of Brittany next to him supporting everything else.

He wanted to touch her, just for a moment, to feel the warmth that radiated from her, to trace the gentle rise and fall of her breasts, to find out if her skin felt as silky as it looked. Slowly, gently, he cupped her foot in one hand.

"Oh, Dunkin, go away," she mumbled in response to his sensuous gesture.

He slid his hand away.

"Are you hungry, boy?" One arm covered her eyes as the blurred words eased from beneath the woolly sleeve.

"Mmm," he grumbled, setting his pipe on the oak coffee table in front of him.

"I thought so," Brittany murmured, her arm falling away as she tugged her eyelids open.

There was a moment of silence. Then she bolted upright. "Sam!"

"In the flesh," he answered with a crooked smile.

As she scurried back toward the end of the couch, Brittany pulled a plump comforter to her chest. She felt naked, exposed somehow. "You—you're here. . . ."

He nodded. "I didn't want to wake you."

"You should have!"

"Why?"

"Because you should have. You shouldn't have watched me sleep. Sleep is private." She was rambling, her thoughts running in and out of the wonderful dream she had been pulled from, a dream filled with the hunk of man sitting at the other end of her couch. Had he somehow pried into them?

"You looked too happy to wake up. I believe we all deserve a romp through dreams now and then."

Romp? Why had he said that? She blushed furiously. "I wasn't dreaming, just sleeping soundly."

He grinned his lopsided grin and angled himself so he faced her fully. She was crouched into the corner of the couch like a little girl, her knees tucked up under her chin and the colorful comforter falling over her and puddling around her feet. Her hair was charmingly mussed and her cheeks flushed. She was beautiful. "Brittany—" His breath caught unexpectedly in his throat. He cleared it and tried again. "Brittany, I needed to check some things with you for the game."

She nodded slowly. "I see."

"And your mother suggested I drive up, since you don't have a phone."

"My mother?"

"Well, she knew I needed the information today. And she said it was an easy drive."

Brittany glanced up at the old hand-carved clock that hung above the fireplace. It was nearly nightfall. "Mother gave you directions . . ." The first hint of a smile played across her lips. "And you got lost."

He nodded. "Well, a little. Your mother is very visual, which is great! But she's not much on road names."

"Mother travels by feel, and it's a foolproof method if she's sitting there beside you. She *never* gets lost."

Brittany's light laughter was music to Sam's ears. He *had* intruded on her privacy, no matter what the excuse. She didn't seem ecstatic to see him, but she wasn't angry. "This copy doesn't need much work, but we wanted you to check it before it went to the printer."

"I'm sorry you had to come all this way. I didn't know you'd be working this weekend."

"Oh, we tend to work crazy hours. And I thought the drive was great. This is a wonderful hideaway you have up here."

She looked around the room and he caught the sadness in her eyes. "I *love* it here," she said slowly. "But it's up for sale, so I'm trying to enjoy it all I can."

"For sale?"

She played with the edge of the comforter. "Yes, no one but me ever comes up here anymore. It's kind of a long trip for Mom and Dad, and Sara never liked the bugs. Gordie never has time. So the only sensible thing to do is to sell it."

"That's too bad." He dropped one hand on her knee and rubbed it gently. Brittany fit in up here, in the natural, untouched beauty, the simpleness of it all. "It's a perfect retreat."

"Yes . . . " She swung her legs over the edge of the couch, her mood changing suddenly to brusqueness.

"Sam, it's late. We ought to go over those things so you can get back to town at a decent hour."

He pulled himself up from the couch. For the first time he noticed how chilly it was in the large room, especially with the sun going down. "Brittany, you're going to be very cold tonight."

"Oh, I was planning on bringing in some wood," she said, brushing her unruly hair back from her face. "But I guess I slept instead."

He reached for his jacket. "I could use a cup of coffee. I'll trade you that for logs. And then we'll get right to work."

When he returned, Brittany had switched on some lamps, put cheese and crackers on the oak table, and the smell of coffee percolating drifted from the kitchen. Straight out of Norman Rockwell, he thought as he hunkered down in front of the fireplace. Domestic bliss. Who would have guessed? It didn't feel bad at all, either. He scratched Dunkin behind the ears, surprised by the curious thought, and began to pile logs into the iron grate.

Brittany appeared from around the corner carrying two cups of coffee and sat down on the couch. "Sam, the radio announced an early-season snow tonight. I think we'd better hurry with whatever you need to show me. You don't want to drive on those narrow roads alone in the snow."

He stared into the leaping flames and nodded. Right, he told himself. Show Brittany the copy, Lawrence, and leave. That's the plan. He gave the logs a final stir, then stood up and joined her on the couch. "You're right, Brittany. Here, this is the copy for the first set of game cards. If you'd just read them over . . . " He slipped several sheets of paper and a pencil out of his tan briefcase and laid them out on the table, then settled back with a mug of coffee warming his hands and watched her. It had taken effort not to touch her.

There was no telling where a touch would go, with the air as heavily charged as it was.

Brittany leaned forward, her brows lifted, and read.

Gordon Winters volunteers for PTA clown; daughters in tears. Go back two spaces.

Kathleen Hunter says "yes" while stuck on top of Ferris wheel. Machinery starts immediately. Collect $200.

Brittany Ellsbeth arrives in middle of board meeting; proud father passes out hunks of stock to all present. Go ahead ten spaces.

Brittany goes out on first date; father accompanies couple and date never returns from men's room at the movie theater. Lose two turns.

Great-uncle Jesse takes Gordon on balloon ride over New Jersey and for the first time in his life runs out of hot air. Go back three squares.

Every now and then Brittany smiled in a way that made Sam, his gaze intent on her profile, smile back. She laid the first sheet down and half-turned to look at him, her eyes misty. "Sam, it's wonderful. Really wonderful. There are so many moments captured here."

"Thanks to you."

"Oh, no, Sam. It's everyone. Why, you've tracked down friends Dad hasn't seen in years. This will mean so much to him."

"Then I've made a believer out of you?"

She nodded slowly, her eyes refocusing on the sheets of paper. Sam had edged closer and his knee brushed her hip as she leaned toward the table. He was wonderfully close. It felt so good, so right.

He slipped one hand around her back and rubbed his thumb teasingly up and down her side.

Busily she picked up another paper and concentrated with all her might on the typed copy, correcting a spelling error here and there, or drumming her fingers thoughtfully on the table.

But Sam's hand wasn't deterred. It slid around until

it found the bottom edge of the shirt that had afforded him such a pleasing view earlier and slipped beneath, sending shivers of delight racing through her body.

"Sam!" she breathed huskily. "I'm trying to work on this."

"Nothing great was ever achieved without passion, Brittany," he murmured into her ear.

With great strength she pulled away and calmed herself, then shuffled the papers neatly into a pile. "There, Sam, all done."

He settled back and pulled out his pipe.

"You know, I've learned a lot about you through all this, Brittany Winters."

"The adventure story of the year!" she joked lightly.

"You've had your share."

"No, Sam. I'm not adventurous at all."

"When you were four years old you got on a bus without being noticed and ended up in Rhode Island. And you never shed a tear. When your parents came to get you, you were doing Shirley Temple dances at the police station."

"Sam! How do you know that?"

"I took Aunt Maggie Winters to tea the other day. She's a wonderful lady with a memory as full and clear as the deep sea." He drew on his pipe, his laughing eyes focused on Brittany. "It appears you're her favorite niece and she seemed far more interested in talking about you than recollecting tales of her successful brother." He leaned forward to cut off two hunks of cheese and handed one to Brittany. "Aunt Maggie liked me, and sees herself as a sort of self-appointed matchmaker."

Brittany laughed carelessly and tossed her head. "That's Aunt Maggie. What else did she tell you?"

"She said you went to Europe."

"I already told you that," Brittany said a little too sharply.

"Yes, you did. Aunt Maggie said you went off with a

sparkle in your eye, an inflatable mattress under your arm, and ready to dance with life." His voice dropped as he watched her closely. He was ready to back off at the slightest indication. But if she wanted to open up to him, he was there. "She said you came back without the mattress, the sparkle was gone, and you weren't dancin' at all."

Her eyes were focused on the flames and she rested her chin in the palm of her hand. Outside, the wind was pushing tiny specks of white up against the windowpanes, but Sam stayed still beside her.

She chose her words carefully. "Yes, I went to Europe as a carefree college girl. And I grew up while I was there." She tilted her head to one side and chanced a look at him. "That happens, Sam. People grow up, sometimes slowly, sometimes quickly."

His brown eyes wordlessly asked more questions, reading into her soul.

She lowered her gaze and went on. "I had a brief, foolish fling in Europe. I met a dashing man who was out to grab the world by the tail. He was charming, fun-loving, a man with dreams that never ended. We shared his flat and lived the life of dreamers, and then he was off one day. Not thoughtlessly. He *did* care about me. But it was his way, and I knew that all along. He left me his flat, all paid for for six months, and even left his Fiat. We said good-bye the way we'd agreed on, happily, thanking each other for the fun we'd had. I guess he was that fond memory all of us has. A first love, that 'being in love with love' time of life." Her voice died away, and she lifted her mug of coffee to her lips. When she started up again, her voice was more distant. "It was so long ago . . . when we waved good-bye . . . "

"And it wasn't quite as easy for you as it was for him?"

She shook her head. "No, I overestimated myself. It wasn't easy at all. But only slightly because of him.

Choices like that—relationships—have consequences. And that's what wasn't easy for me."

He wanted to pull her close and soothe the sadness in her eyes away. Wanted to shake the dreamer in her past for daring to hurt this woman. Wanted to make everything better. But he knew he couldn't. Brittany needed to let that sadness out in her own way, to release it. So instead, he waited patiently, his hand gently rubbing the tenseness out of the small of her back. Her eyes told him there was more, but after a moment she turned and forced a smile to her lips. "You've played your tricks on me again. I don't like to talk about myself."

"Maybe you should talk about yourself more often," he said. "Sometimes real demons are exorcised through words."

She shook her head. "No demons, Sam. Nothing more to say. Except— Oh, my Lord, Sam. Look!" She set her mug down with a thud and pointed toward the window, her eyes wide.

The darkness beyond the window was now a flurry of dancing white flakes, flattening into a soft unbroken blanket against the windowpane.

He smiled calmly. "First snowfall. That's good luck, you know."

Brittany was off the couch and moving toward the window. "You'll have to drive in this . . ." She turned back to him, her brows drawing together. "What do you mean, good luck?"

"If one is in the company of a beautiful woman during the first snowfall, one's year will be blessed with much joy." He was right beside her now, his hand resting on her shoulder as he watched the whirling mass of snowflakes beyond the pane.

"I have a suspicion you made that up, Sam. But I do hope it brings you good luck on your way home. . . ." She didn't want him to leave, she realized suddenly. For once she didn't want the solitude, the meditative silence, the time to think. But she knew she couldn't ask him to stay, either. "Oh, Sam, I'm sorry. If I hadn't talked so much, you would have left long ago."

"Not a chance." He rubbed her shoulders and continued to look out into the darkness. She had opened up a little, like a flower beginning to blossom. And he knew he couldn't force the opening any more than he could with a flower. But there'd been a start . . .

"Brittany." He gently turned her toward him. "I guess I had better go. I know you came out here to get away."

She looked up at him and said nothing.

He smiled, then walked back to the couch and slipped the papers into his briefcase. "I do appreciate your doing this—"

With her back to the window, she watched him move purposefully around the room, putting on his jacket, preparing to leave.

"Maybe a cup of coffee to go with you . . . ?" she asked, taking a step toward him.

He shook his head. "Nope. I wouldn't mind a safe-driving kiss, though. They say it brings good luck."

Laughing, she walked over to him. She kissed him on the lips, then pulled away quickly. "Drive carefully, Sam." On these winding unknown roads, a little voice in her head said, in the dark, and with the snow settling on his windows . . . "Oh, Sam."

"Yes, Brittany?" He had his hand on the door, his fingers turning the knob.

"You can't go," she said quietly.

Sam studied her face, trying to sort out the tangled emotions he saw there. Concern . . . desire . . . fear . . . But it was the concern, he knew, that made her ask him to stay. "I'll be all right."

"But I'd worry all night—and there's no way you can call me to tell me you've arrived safely." She was at his side now, her hand resting on his arm.

"You're sure?"

"I'm sure. There are four bedrooms upstairs, for heaven's sake. And we're certainly adults."

"Certainly." He slipped out of his jacket and flung it over the back of the chair. "Not only that, but I've proof of honor." He pulled out his wallet and extracted a card from it. "Here. You can keep this under your pillow."

She took the thin card from him and looked at it carefully, then burst into laughter. "Sam Lawrence, an eagle scout?"

"Yes, ma'am. At your service." He saluted, then took her by the shoulders and turned her toward the room. "But first things first, madame. I'm about to fall over from hunger. Lead me to the kitchen and I shall make you a feast most people only *dream* about."

"And cooked by an eagle scout!"

"*And* an altar boy, but we didn't get cards for that."

She looked at him sideways. "Little did I dream . . ."

"And there's more to come, my love. Let us feast and make merry. And let it snow, let it snow, let it snow!"

His deep baritone echoed through the room and Brittany followed him into the kitchen with wings on her heels, a gentle happiness blooming in every secret part of her.

Eight

"Oh, Sam," Brittany moaned as she walked over to the refrigerator, her socks slipping on the smooth floor.

"No, don't say it. You don't have any food." He and Dunkin were close behind her.

"I picked up some vegetables on my way in, and I was going to go to the store after I brought in the wood." She pulled the door open and looked in dismay at the sparse contents.

"But you fell asleep."

She nodded. He bent and looked over her shoulder into the cool interior, his chin tickling her shoulder as he did a quick inventory.

"Hmm. Well, don't worry, my lovely Brittany. They don't call me Improvisational Sam for nothing." With great flair he swept her over to a high stool beside the large cooking island, then returned to rummage through the refrigerator with the finesse of a Julia Child. "Okay. Fine. Yes, this will do quite nicely. Perfect!"

She watched as he pulled things out of the refrigerator and plopped them on the counter. It was the only right and decent thing to have him stay, she told herself as he began chopping an onion. And it did feel good to have a man in the house. No, face it Brittany. What feels good is having Sam Lawrence in the house.

Sam finished cutting the onion, several mushrooms, half a tomato, and a green pepper, then grated some cheddar cheese. He could feel Brittany relaxing by the minute, and that pleased him enormously. Her uneasiness and reticence crept in at odd moments, and he wanted nothing more right now than to assure her that there was no way on God's earth he would hurt her. He'd keep the mood light, keep the worry from her eyes. Keep everything easy and relaxed . . . "Okay, Brittany, here we go. We have here, m'lady, the makings for Samson's super omelet."

"Samson!" She covered her grin with one hand.

He feigned hurt as he cracked the eggs into a bowl. "Of course. That biblical fellow with the strength and dashing good looks."

"Well, that's good to know. Should things get out of hand, all I need is a scissors to lop off that head of hair of yours. . . ." Her gaze fell on his thick brown hair falling askew over one eye as he stirred the creamy yellow mixture, then poured it into a frying pan. It was wonderful hair, wonderful to run her hands through. "And all strength will be gone," she finished weakly.

He began tossing the other ingredients into the pan. "No, that's where *that* Samson and I differ." He looked over at her and smiled a slow, devastating smile. "My strengths are in all sorts of hidden places. But you're more than welcome to look for them, Brittany."

She choked. "That—omelet smells good." She quickly uncorked a bottle of wine and poured two glasses.

"Good? Brittany dear, this is a *magic* omelet, not adequately described by a mere adjective such as 'good.' This omelet is guaranteed to make you lust for it the rest of your natural days!" He flipped the omelet neatly onto one of the plates she had set out, cut it in two, and set half on the other plate. "I make the best omelet east of the Rockies." He paused for a moment. "Hell, probably west too."

"Such modesty, Mr. Lawrence! Well, it better be good or the yolk will be on you."

He laughed at her silly pun and helped her pile everything onto a large pewter tray. "I'll properly ignore that. Now, dear Brittany, shall we retire to the warmth of the fire to savor these gourmet wonders?"

In minutes they were both settled comfortably in front of the leaping flames, their backs supported by plump, oversized pillows, their plates balanced expertly on their laps.

Sam watched her carefully as she slid a forkful of the rich, moist omelet between her lips. "Well? What do you think?"

"You're absolutely right." She wiped a trace of egg from the corner of her mouth. "Best in the east *and* west."

He beamed. "Now I'm convinced you have wonderful taste." He reached over and walked his fingers lazily across her hand.

She eyed him warily, then slipped her hand away to reach for her wineglass. She took a quick sip. "You know, Sam, we have a dog at Petpals who's a lot like you."

He laughed huskily. "He cooks?"

"No. He begs . . . for attention. And I usually throw him shoes."

He grabbed her foot, rubbing the thick sock over her toes until she wriggled with pleasure. "Shoes . . . socks . . . anything will do."

"You're impossible." She finished her omelet and set her plate down, then wrapped her arms around her knees. "But impossible or not, Sam, I'm still glad you stayed."

He poured more wine for them both, then lifted his glass and clinked it lightly against hers. "Here's to those who stay. . . ."

Their eyes met and held as they swallowed the wine. "To those who stay . . ." she repeated softly.

She glanced at the nearly empty bottle of wine and pressed one palm to her cheek. "Sam, are you trying to get me drunk?" she asked teasingly.

He shook his head, watching the firelight cast a glow on her cheeks. "Eagle scout . . . remember?"

"My brother Gordie was an eagle scout. And at the awards ceremony one of the older eagle scouts tried to squeeze my thigh underneath the punch and cookie table."

"Did he succeed?"

She laughed. "No. I managed to lower my hand holding a chocolate eclair just as he made his move, and he got a handful of *it* instead."

He poured the rest of the wine into their glasses. "Sounds like you've always been able to take care of yourself just fine, Brittany."

"Most of the time I do all right." A shadow passed over her eyes, but disappeared almost as quickly as it came.

"Brittany?" He slid closer and slipped his arm around her shoulders. "What's wrong?"

"Nothing, I'm fine. A little hazy, perhaps." She leaned her head back and it settled naturally on his shoulder. "But otherwise just fine."

Her lashes fell like butterfly wings onto her cheeks and she sat still for so long, Sam thought maybe she had fallen asleep. An angel asleep in his arms, he thought, his fingers gently combing her hair. And she fit just right. As he moved his hand slightly, her hair swept against his cheek, and the clean, fresh smell of her filled his senses. She was so soft and wonderful. So delicately sensual. So . . . He swallowed with great difficulty, then his whole body tensed.

"Brittany, wake up." He shook her lightly but firmly.

"Sam!" Her eyes opened wide. "What's wrong?"

"Nothing. I think we ought to go outside, that's all."

Because if he didn't, right this minute, he might burn his eagle scout card!

"Outside?" Was he crazy? she thought. She hadn't been asleep at all, just quietly absorbing every small feel and smell of Sam Lawrence. Basking in it, tasting it in her mind, then carefully committing it to memory.

"Yes, outside." He was already standing, pulling her to her feet. "That good-luck spell doesn't work unless you actually touch the snow. Come on."

She stared at his back as he headed for the door. The man was totally unpredictable. Wasn't he enjoying the moment of closeness too? She slipped into her shoes and pulled on her jacket, then quickly went out the door after him. Maybe she just didn't understand men.

"Ah." Sam lifted his face and let the filmy snowflakes settle on his cheeks. "Wonderful!"

"Inside was wonderful too," she whispered.

"The air feels so good." He stretched his arms wide and breathed deeply, his lungs expanding and the cold air calming his body. He wrapped one arm around Brittany and held her close.

Brittany gazed out into the fairy-tale night. The snow was polka-dotted against the inky darkness and barely covered the tall pine trees and fence posts. Along the ground was a thin graceful wave of white. It *was* beautiful . . . a beautiful snowy night, and a wonderful man standing close beside her. As the cold air began to penetrate, her head cleared and the dreamy, foggy sensation lifted. But not the feeling of utter happiness that swept through her again and again, like a swiftly flowing river. It was Sam, standing there beside her. He was turning a lovely night into something far more. And with firm determination, she blocked out rational thought and refused to let its icy logic ruin the first snow.

"In the dead of winter the snow piles as high as a man's head out here," she said, looking out toward the dark woods.

"How high?"

"Up to here." She reached up and rubbed one hand across the top of his head, her fingers touching the snowflakes that had settled there.

She grinned and dropped her head back to catch the snowflakes on the tip of her tongue like she used to as a child. "Do we make a wish?"

He looked down at her. "I think the good luck comes naturally now. No wish necessary." With the tip of one finger he touched a lacy snowflake that had settled on the tip of her nose, then bent and kissed it away.

Her eyes were open, soft and flecked with tiny lights. The fear was gone, the anxiousness he'd seen earlier, and left was a wonderful warmth. It held him silent for a full minute, a minute touched with night magic. "Brittany, you're going to have to stop looking at me like that," he said, his words coming out with difficulty.

When she shook her head, tiny snowflakes fell from her hair like fairy dust. "I can't," she said simply.

"Then I can't be responsible."

"I reached the age of reason long ago, Sam." Her voice, low and husky, stirred the embers he had tried so hard to smother, and his arm grew tighter around her shoulder, his fingers pressing into her arm.

"You're doing crazy things to me . . ."

"Kiss me, Sam."

"Yes," he whispered, his breath blowing gently on her parted lips as he brought his mouth down possessively onto hers.

The sky faded out and the earth lost its feel for Brittany as she clung to him, letting his gently probing tongue and the lovely pressure of his mouth fill her with wonder. She answered him fully, her lips fitting to his as one, perfectly. They separated only long enough to breathe in tiny gulps of air, then joined again. This time they both felt a growing urgency wrapping itself around them.

Brittany reached up and circled his neck with her

arms, pressing her body against his, clinging there and willing away reason. One night, one beautiful night. Surely she could handle that much. "Sam, may we go back in now? And don't worry about protecting me. I'm a big girl." Her words were spoken softly, but he didn't miss a single one.

He looked down at her, but she had already slipped her arms from his neck and was turning back, one hand reaching for his as she guided him into the house.

Wordlessly, they removed their jackets and moved back to the fire. Sam poked it into life, then drew Brittany down in front of it. The warmth returned.

"Here's to our good-luck snow," he said. He slipped her wine into her shaking hand and clinked his glass against it.

They drank silently, reading the growing desire in each other's eyes. Brittany was overwhelmed with feeling for this incredible man who was so gentle with her, so caring. Surely no pain could come from that. She set her glass down on the raised stone hearth and watched the firelight shine in his eyes.

"Do you see yourself there, in my eyes?" he asked huskily.

She nodded.

"And how do you look?"

"Cloudy, starry-eyed."

His arms wrapped around her and he shifted until she was cradled between his bent legs, her back to his front. "That's how you make me feel, Brittany. Cloudy . . . and a little bit in awe of this feeling."

She nodded, gazing at the brilliant orange and yellow spears of fire dancing in the fireplace. They seemed to leap from the fireplace right into her, shooting through every inch of her.

"I'm in awe too, Sam. I didn't intend to feel this way about you. But I do, and it's about as controllable as those flames. It's—it's all through me, Sam, a forest fire, out of control." She rubbed her head back and forth against his cheek.

He nipped softly at her neck as he felt the passion unleash within her. He ran his palms down the length of her arms, his chin tucked closely into the crook of her neck as he, too, stared at the fire. "Have you ever noticed how sensuous the flames in a fire are, Brittany? They dance and curl and twine about each other. . . ."

The flames *were* like dancers, she thought as she tried to control her heartbeat. And it was a love dance they were doing, winding and twirling, the colors changing just like the myriad sensations sweeping through her. She was lifted by a rush of warmth, then light shivers ran through her, then she was bathed in moist desire. She wet her lips and pressed back into the V of his body.

His hard thighs tightened instinctively around her, locking her against his body and sending a whole new wave of feelings surging through her.

She could feel the hard heat of his arousal pressed into her back, could feel the strong, quick beat of his heart, and she savored the heat that seared her at each point of contact. Her whole body was strangely alive with the sensations that leaped as powerfully as the flames in front of her.

Behind her Sam sensed her excitement and desire. His own was just barely controlled. He slipped his hands down to the edge of her shirt and stroked his thumbs across the soft, creamy skin beneath. It was warm and silky and alive to his touch.

"It's getting warm," she murmured.

He kissed the crook of her neck. "Here, this'll help." The bottom button slipped open easily, and he continued all the way to the top, his fingers sure as they rubbed against her skin, his hands reassuring. He parted the fabric and gently cupped her ribs with his large hands, his fingers creating wonderful patterns as he slowly massaged her skin.

She sighed as pleasure filled her. Sam was so sure,

so tender, that she barely felt it when he undid the front snap of her bra and slipped it aside.

Sam's breath caught as he looked down at the creamy curves of her breasts. Her skin was flawless, her breasts full and firm as they rose and fell with soft pressure into his palms.

He'd dreamed of this, of holding her like this, but she was far more beautiful in reality, far lovelier than any fantasy he could have created in his mind. "Oh, Brittany, you're so lovely."

With the grace of the dancing flames he moved from behind her and stretched out along the floor, drawing her down in front of him after he effortlessly eased her out of the flannel shirt and bra. "The fire will warm you," he whispered into her hair.

"My handsome, loving eagle scout," she murmured.

She lay there, half naked, feeling no fear or alarm or inhibition as his gaze took in the lovely contours of her breasts. She felt only happiness with this man who cradled her head gently against his forearm and looked down lovingly into her eyes.

He abandoned his own shirt on the couch and her gaze rested on the marvelous thatch of tawny-colored hair that covered his broad chest, glistening with tiny beads of moisture. It was the same Sam who had come to her in her dreams, leaving her reluctantly at dawn. But he was here, really here. She reached up and touched the blond curls, twisting them lightly between her fingers. "Oh, Sam," she murmured dreamily, "you're so beautiful."

"*We're* beautiful, Brittany. Together."

"I'm drifting, Sam. I'm in another world. . . ."

"It's the omelet, Brittany. I didn't mention its side effects, I guess." His husky laughter touched her heart.

"I . . . would . . . like . . . that . . . recipe," she managed weakly as she moistened her lips.

"We can probably improve on it if we work at it." His fingers moved playfully across her breasts, and he watched as the pale brown nipples tightened and grew firm beneath his touch. Her soft moan was music lighting his soul. "You're so beautiful, my darling, lovely Brittany. So beautiful . . ."

His head dipped until he touched each breast with his lips, first one, then the other, slowly tasting the sweetness of her flesh until her body writhed beneath his hot tongue. "Oh, Sam—" she cried, tangling her hands in his hair as his head moved lower, tracing a hot moist trail down her stomach.

She bit on her lip, unable to fathom the depths of her pleasure. She knew she was in paradise, and she didn't ever want to leave.

Sam lifted his head and ran his hand over her, slowly moving lower, covering every inch of her stomach in warm strokes until his fingers touched the top of her jeans. They rested there for just a fraction of a moment before unsnapping the clasp and lowering the zipper, then slipping beneath the material. He could feel her consent, and understood simply and surely that she wanted him to know all of her.

A hot sweetness spread like wild honey down to her loins, and she felt moist and weightless all through her body. It had been so long. A huge rush of happiness, so powerful it brought tears to her eyes, swept over her.

He saw her tender expression and paused. "Brittany . . . ?"

Her hair floated around her shoulders as she nodded, one tear trailing in slow motion down her cheek. "Oh, Sam. Dear, dear, Sam. I want you so very much. . . ."

"You're sure, Brittany?"

"It's probably the only thing in my life right now I know for sure."

His smile filled her as his fingers continued exploring beneath her jeans, caressing her abdomen, rubbing across her hips. With the strength of his namesake he peeled the denim and silky panties down her long slender legs, leaving them in a pile at her feet. In another single movement he joined them with his own. "There . . ."

He gazed at her stretched out before him, his eyes traveling the full length of her body, and he couldn't speak. She was incredibly lovely, soft and perfect and beautiful.

Forcing breath into his lungs, he leaned on one elbow and traced a path up her body with his hand, slowly roaming over her creamy skin. The desire to please Brittany, to bring her to ecstasy with him, was so enormous a need, it nearly overwhelmed him. It wasn't a selfish quest as it sometimes was. Brittany was too important, too special, already too much a part of him for him to think of her in any casual way.

He slipped one hand between her legs and sought the tender flesh of her inner thighs. It was silky and smooth and his fingers slid sensuously over it until he could feel the delight surging through her.

"Oh, Sam . . ." Her eyes shut as she seemed to spin above the earth. "Your touch is as magical as your omelets."

"It's the one I'm touching who's magical." His hand moved to stroke the gentle slope of her hip, then slipped on down until it brought all of her body into full and astonishing bloom.

"Oh, Sam, my Sam. I love you." Her arms reached up and curled around his neck as she released the pent-up love that had been threatening to explode inside her. It had been there for many days now, pushed down deep where no one could see it and she didn't have to think about it. But beneath Sam's gaze and loving caresses, nothing was secret anymore.

"I love you, Brittany," he whispered back.

She clung to him, pulling him down until his body lay heavily on her own, until the hot hardness of his desire pressed against her skin and his lips finally met hers in a loving and passionate kiss that seemed to suck every tiny ounce of breath out of both of them.

Before his desire raged out of control, Sam pushed himself slightly away from her. "My, oh, my, Brittany Ellsbeth Winters, you sure can kiss," he whispered thickly.

"Sam, I do want you. . . ." Her eyes were dewy, the golden flecks brighter than firelight. And for the first time since meeting Brittany those few weeks before, Sam saw no fear in those magical eyes.

Brittany moved her hands from his shoulders to the springy thatch of hair, then slid her palms down the wide expanse of his chest. She wanted desperately to know every inch of him, to tuck it all away in her memory. The plane of his abdomen was flat and hard. She kneaded it lightly, pressing, wanting to get closer and closer until there was nothing left between them, nothing to keep her separate from him.

When her hands continued exploring, he moaned helplessly, his body moving to the rhythm of her, wanting her more than breath or life itself.

"Brittany, be mine." He lowered his body over hers, his hands moving up to cradle her head. "I want to love you, my beautiful, special Brittany."

Tiny kisses covered his face in reply as she pulled him close, and when he finally eased himself into her, she arched her back in joyful welcome, crying out her love in total, complete abandon.

Her face glowed with dazed delight as he moved within her, and the love pouring from her eyes sent him to deeper and deeper depths, until neither heaven nor earth could stop the enormous explosion of love that sent them soaring together above snow-kissed pines and into a galaxy of their own.

The bed was soft as a cloud, cradling her body and lulling it back to earth. Brittany stretched one arm across the downy comforter and smiled a joyful smile in her sleep.

Sam was leaning lazily on one elbow, watching in

wonder her every move, every expression that flickered across her face. He found watching Brittany sleep fascinating, and loved the tiny changes that moved her eyelids or twitched her lips.

He wondered if she even knew she was in bed. She'd been sound asleep in front of the fire, her limbs tangled deliciously with his, when the fire had finally died and he'd lifted her carefully in his arms and carried her off to bed.

He hadn't seen the bedrooms before and didn't know if he had the right one or not, but it didn't matter. At the top of the stairs he'd found a large airy room with a wonderful four-poster that seemed just right. He and Brittany fit together in it perfectly and that was all that mattered in the world.

Now the filtered light of morning was falling on her in soft, slanted lines and he found himself wanting to record this time because it was far more special than any other morning in his life.

"You're doing it again," a faint voice murmured.

"What, love?" He leaned closer to catch the muffled sounds.

Her eyelids didn't move. "You're watching me, Sam. Watching me sleep."

"Mmm." He kissed each lid. "And I'm finding out wonderful things about you while you sleep."

"Oh?" One brow rose slowly.

He nodded and moved his hand to tease the pale rise of breast just visible above the edge of the sheet. "Your breathing is as soft as a kitten's purr, and you smile at dawn."

She shivered. "I do?"

"You do." He smiled as his fingers continued their sensuous travels.

"What else do I do, Sam?" Her husky voice stirred him and he felt a familiar tightening between his loins.

"Things like this. . . ." He lifted her hand and rested

it on his chest, then rotated it downward in slow, lazy circles.

She was wide awake now, her eyes open and a tiny smile playing around her lips. "I didn't . . ."

He just nodded, capturing her heart again with the loving smile that spilled from his eyes. "But then I did this." He slipped back the sheet and cupped her breast in his hand, slowly teasing it to hardness. "And this." His lips lowered and sought hers hungrily, tasting her, wanting her, loving her.

"Oh, Sam," she said breathlessly as she finally inched away from him and looked with pure longing into his eyes. "You dropped into my life when I wasn't looking. And now that you're here, I don't know quite what to do with you."

"Love me," he said quietly.

And she did.

Nine

The early snow had covered the whole valley in quiet isolation.

When Brittany pulled her eyes open again hours later, the only sound in her room was that of a clean wind blowing through the pine trees and soft footsteps coming up the stairs.

Sam peeked his head around the corner. "Well, and the top of the mornin' to you, sleeping beauty." He walked on into the room carrying a large wicker tray. The most delicious aromas she had smelled in a lifetime wafted from it.

"Sam . . ." She smiled as she pushed herself up against the soft pillows, the sheet tucked neatly beneath her arms. Sam, who'd moved from her dreams to the doorway, and now walked slowly toward her through the muted morning sunlight. She blinked once to assure herself he wasn't a vision. No, he was still there, every wonderful inch of him. He wore nothing but his blue jeans, the faded denim hung low on hips she had caressed. She swallowed hard and tore her gaze away from his tantalizing body to look up into his smiling brown eyes.

He was watching her watch him with obvious enjoyment.

"Sam, it's you," she said at last, the words hanging limply in the air.

"You were, perhaps, expecting the butler?" He drew his brows together and stiffened his body into his best servant pose, puffing out his broad chest.

Her sleepy laughter echoed through the room. "No, but I thought it might be just another incredible dream and I'd wake up with nothing but lovely memories."

He slid the tray onto the bedside table and sat down next to her. "Does this feel like a memory?" he growled, one hand sliding beneath the cool sheet as he dipped his head and kissed her shoulder.

She could only shake her head, her breasts trembling at his touch.

"Or this?" He lifted his head to kiss awake each eyelid, then met her lips fully and lovingly. He couldn't seem to get enough of her, the sight and smell and wonderful feel of her naked body. He remembered the sound of her sensual laughter as it had laced through their lovemaking, the way she had touched him and loved him. "I don't think any dream or fantasy could compete with us, my darling Brittany."

She spread one hand out across his chest and looked deeply into his eyes. "No, I don't either, Sam."

He sat still for a minute, reining in the desire to pull back the sheets, to love her again and again and again.

"What did you bring in with you?" she finally managed to ask, her own desire barely restrained.

"Breakfast, my love." He smiled and lifted the overladen tray to the side of the bed.

She eyed it in disbelief. "Sam," she said slowly, "there wasn't enough food left in my refrigerator to fill a coffee cup, much less that tray."

"You're a very astute, perceptive lady. That's just one of the many things I love about you." He kissed the top of her head, then sat down beside the tray.

"Where then?" She lifted the linen napkin and uncovered a basket of flaky croissants that smelled like they'd just emerged from the oven. Beneath a lid was a huge Belgium waffle, filled with sour cream and strawberries, and perfectly browned sausages. "Oh, Sam . . ."

"I deserve most of the credit, but not all of it," he said modestly. "Kendrick's bakery supplied the croissants and I persuaded Mr. Jackson from the market next door to open early so I could get the groceries. The rest is simply magic." He winked and lifted a mug of steaming coffee into her hands.

"You went into town?"

He nodded. "But it was too early to call Gary with those changes, so you and I'll have to go back later to ring him up, as they say over in Evergreen."

"Sam . . ." She looked down at the delicious breakfast and her heart swelled. "You're quite wonderful, you know."

He simply watched her, his own heart filled with feelings that were strange and new and completely unexpected. They were far more complex than any game he had ever put together or puzzle he had solved, but the overriding joy with which this woman filled him was argument enough that the feelings were well worth figuring out.

After eating and showering and dressing in heavy wool sweaters that Brittany had unearthed from a large cedar closet, they were ready to find a telephone.

"There's an old inn through the woods that's closer than town," Brittany said, "and it's a wonderful walk."

She grabbed his hand and they walked out the back door, heading for the woods.

The world was silent, coated with a gentle powdering of snow, the air crisp and lovely, and above it all the sun shone brightly.

Brittany couldn't control the smile that crept across

her face without notice or provocation. So this was what the songs were about, and movies made, and books written, she thought. It was glorious! "A near perfect day, wouldn't you say, Mr. Lawrence?"

He looked down into her shining eyes and drew her close. "You better watch the way you look at me, young lady, or we'll never make it through these woods!"

"Hmmm." She looked around at the matted leaves, then shook her head. "No, I guess it's too wet here."

His deep laughter spun sunshine through her heart. "Brittany Ellsbeth Winters, I'm surprised at you!"

"You've released a demon in me, Sam." She growled playfully and hugged him.

The flirting was something new, a dangling of her womanhood out there in front of him, and he delighted in it.

"An angel," he corrected her softly. "A lovely, sensuous spirit that surely came straight from heaven." He breathed in the lovely smell of her hair and walked on, marveling at how perfectly she fit there at his side, more perfect than the parts of his games or the pieces of a puzzle. The canopy of branches laced over them, and they walked on quietly in the muted light, basking in the special feelings that their lovemaking had woven about them.

"Are these woods a part of your property?" Sam asked presently.

"Yes. The land was my grandfather's, and it included the inn we're going to. But Dad sold off that part of it years ago. My grandfather's caretaker and his wife bought it and run it all year round."

They continued walking together with the ease born of their intimacy. When the path narrowed and his hip rubbed against hers, she wound her arm around his waist and held him close. No words were needed to speak her happiness.

She noticed Sam's easy happiness too. He held her to him, and dropped kisses in her hair when he ducked beneath overhanging branches. It was all as natural as the untouched dew that surrounded them.

"Cold?" he asked at one point.

"No." She'd never be cold again. The warmth Sam had filled her with had to be enough to last an entire lifetime.

"Smell, Sam. Smell these woods. Isn't it wonderful? It's the smell of my childhood and my youth. Every season has its own specialness, the fragrant newness of spring and the delicious, pungent leaves in the fall."

"But not nearly as delicious as you." He nuzzled the side of her neck until she giggled helplessly.

"But you're right, Brittany, it's a grand place."

"And wait until you see the inn. I know you'll be crazy about it too."

She loved sharing this place with Sam, loved having him breathe in the same scents and hear the same woodland noises that had always brought her such joy. She looked around and wondered fleetingly if it could ever be the same here alone. Solitary walks through these woods had always been special to her. Now *alone* seemed full of emptiness.

But the thought didn't fit into the beautiful day and she quickly banished it as she squeezed Sam's waist and directed him onto the path that led to the inn.

A gust of wind riffled through her hair and as she brushed it back, her eyes shifted up to Sam's face. At first his gaze seemed focused on the line of white cedar trees in the distance, but when she looked closer, she saw he was looking far beyond the trees and the woods. He was looking at something not within her sight, but much farther away. Another world, or a dream? The future?

She breathed in deeply to calm the disturbing effects of her thoughts and rubbed her cheek gently against the nubby gray wool of his sweater. He was here now and that was all that mattered today. She pressed one mittened hand against his cheek, and when he smiled down at her she reached up and kissed him with an intensity that stilled the trembling of her lips and poured the warmth back into her limbs and her heart.

He responded immediately, his arms wrapping around her and his lips savoring the wonder of her.

"My woodland nymph," he murmured. "I wish this could go on forever."

She smiled and hoped he wouldn't notice the moisture in her eyes. She'd give all she owned in the world if what he said could be true. A frozen moment in time. With forced lightness she shook her head and laughed. "Behave yourself. We're here, you see. Civilization has intruded."

The path broadened until finally the trees fell back and in the distance they saw the sprawling three-story inn standing grandly on a slight rise against the wintry sky. It was nearly picture-perfect, with the dusting of snow not yet melted, the freshly painted barns, and a horsedrawn carriage sitting on the circle drive in front of the inn.

Sam whistled softly through his teeth. "You know, Brittany, I've been to a lot of places, but you're introducing me to a kind of beauty that I haven't seen matched."

"Isn't it all in the eye of the beholder?" she half-teased, leading him through a small grove of trees and around to the front porch. "Perhaps you're ready for this *kind* of beauty now, something without grandeur, just simple and natural."

"Or perhaps you enhance what I see."

"Perhaps . . ." She smiled again, then directed her attention back to the inn. "My grandfather said this was a tavern years ago." She pointed up to the third floor with its shuttered windows and tiny porches. "And whatever went on on that third floor made it more popular than the general store."

Sam laughed as he hugged her. "Want me to venture a guess? They probably needed a way to keep warm through the New England winters. I know a better arrangement, how about you?"

She tilted her head back and her eyes met his, sharing lovers' laughter. "Me, too, but I'll never tell." She clasped his hand in her soft mitten and walked on.

Sam's gaze moved beyond the house to a scooped out area down near the edge of the east woods. "What's that?"

Her eyes lit up. "That's where I learned to ice skate. They'll flood it soon and put up small warming sheds for the guests."

"I never learned to ice skate," he mused almost to himself. In his mind he could see laughing children and couples with their arms linked together gliding over the ice. "Maybe sometime we can try it."

It was a vague statement, but Brittany heard it and tucked it away. *Maybe . . . sometime . . .*

"You know, Sam," she said as they mounted the wide snow-covered steps to the inn, "sometimes I think I love it here because it's so unreal. So picture-perfect."

"You mean like an escape?"

She nodded.

"I guess it could be that," he said thoughtfully, gazing at the snow-tipped trees that rose in lines along the hill beyond the house. "Sometimes escapes aren't all bad. I do my share of that. As long as we come back to real life in the end, it's okay, the way I see it."

And this weekend, Brittany wondered, was it an escape? And then in the end they'd come back to real life? To Sam chasing his rainbows and to her settling into her carefully planned days and nights. She sighed, knowing that whatever happened, she'd never be able to live in quite the same way. She was different because of Sam, no matter what.

The inn was bustling quietly with guests and Brittany showed Sam into the paneled library to make his call, then left him alone while she sought out her friends, Ida and Jack Plunkett, who ran the inn.

When he was finished repeating the copy corrections to Gary, Sam hung up the phone and looked approvingly around the library. Comfortable, well-used chairs, enough books to get one through a dozen snowy winters, and a fireplace piled high with kindling and fat logs. He shoved his hands deep into his pockets and sighed contentedly. He'd stayed in elegant European homes, in hotels the size of small towns, in cottages along the Rhine, but nothing had prepared him for the improbable warmth he was finding here in these Maine woods. Or was it Brittany Ellsbeth Winters? Brittany . . . *his* Brittany. He shook his head, but the sensation didn't clear. The feeling that was rooting him to the plank floor overtook him with a vengeance now. Hell, this wasn't a game at all. It wasn't even funny. Being in love didn't fit in any of life's categories he had explored thus far. Uncharted woods, he thought. Guess it was time to do a little charting.

"There you are." A portly woman with sparkling blue eyes walked into the room and scattered Sam's thoughts. "I'm Ida Plunkett, and you must be the Sam that's been lighting sparks in our Brittany's eyes. I'm so happy to meet you!"

The smile returned to his face in a flash and he strode over to meet Ida Plunkett.

He shook her hand warmly, met her laughing eyes, and made a friend.

"We haven't seen Brittany in some time," Ida confided. "And she's never brought a friend before. This is quite nice for all of us. Now, come."

She had Sam by the arm and was leading him through a wide hallway then into the kitchen, where a jumble of happy voices greeted him.

"Hi, Sam, come on in!" Brittany sat at a round oak table in the huge country kitchen, a curly-haired baby bouncing up and down on her knee. The chorus of voices that echoed her invitation came from tiny and not so tiny mouths covered with jam and honey. "Meet Ida and Jack's grandchildren."

The five kids grinned between bites as they were introduced and Ida ushered Sam to an empty chair beside Brittany.

"Quite a brood, Ida," he said. He rubbed the tousled hair of Henry, who was eight, and graciously took an offered bite of shy six-year-old Danny's apple. "An admirable dynasty, to say the least."

Ida nodded, loving each one with a twinkling smile. "They live over in Evergreen but spend lots of time here. I think it's my buttermilk biscuits that keeps 'em coming back." She stepped around a tiny puppy licking up the crumbs and slipped a basketful beneath Sam's nose. "Now, you tell me if they're worth coming back for, Sam."

He swallowed one in a single bite. "Ida, I'm staying. For a few years or maybe forever. Henry, pass the honey please."

"Me, too," Danny promptly agreed, sidling up to Sam and offering his approval. "I'm staying forever. Me and Sam."

Ida laughed and tweaked Danny's ear with grandmotherly affection. "That will be just fine with us. Which reminds me of more serious things, Brittany dear. We've had several interested nibbles on your place."

Brittany's smile faded. "Well, I guess that's good, Ida." She concentrated on the toddler in her lap, tickling her fat tummy. "I'll tell Dad when I get back. He's greatly relieved you're handling the sale for him. He didn't want an agency doing it that might turn it into Lord knows what."

"Well, dear, your father has been more than good to us, you know. It pains us to have that property change hands, though. It just doesn't seem right to Jack and me, even though we know it makes sense, and of course there will always be rooms ready for you here." She shook her head and briskly wiped her hands off on her apron. "I do need you to look at the description we wrote up before you leave. Maybe I could get it now . . ."

Brittany nodded as she frowned down at the infant. "Oh-oh. It'll have to wait, Ida, I think Missy here needs me more."

Henry wrinkled his nose. "Missy's her own rain forest, Pop says." The other kids giggled while Ida fished a diaper out of the large plastic bag on the counter and handed it to Brittany. "You don't mind, dear?"

"Here." Sam held out his arms to Missy, who immediately gurgled her consent. He captured the tiny round body in his large hands and held her secure. "My turn. Hello, beautiful." He smiled charmingly at the baby.

"Sam," Brittany started to argue.

"Hey, you go look at those papers with Ida. And don't be so sexist about this, you'll give the kids a bad example. Come on, gang, I'll give you all a lesson in efficiency here."

Brittany shrugged, but snuck glances over her shoulder as Sam scooted his chair back, rested the wriggling baby girl on his long lap, and whipped the diaper out of its folds. "Okay, gang," he instructed with exaggerated authority and a giant wink, "first you make sure we're talking rain forest here and not the more serious stuff." The kids giggled hilariously as Sam twisted his face into a variety of expressions and expertly relieved Missy of her dampened diaper.

Ida handed her a piece of paper and she skimmed the description of the house. "That's fine, Ida," she said distractedly, still snatching amazed looks at the group huddled around Sam's knees.

"And don't you worry about the place," Ida said. "Jack will keep an eagle eye on it and we'll plow the drive as always."

Brittany drew her attention back to the gentle innkeeper. "Oh, I know you will. Thank you." She hugged

Ida impulsively, wrapping her arms tight around the soft, plump form.

Ida smiled into Brittany's hair and patted her gently on the back. She knew what the hug and emotion were all about, even if Brittany didn't. Had nothing to do with plowing a drive, that was for sure! She knew Brittany Ellsbeth was finally, wholeheartedly in love. With gentle affection she pulled away and looked over her shoulder at Sam. He was playing pattycake with the baby while teaching the others a string trick with Jenny's hair ribbon. Uh-huh. And *he* was over the edge too. Fine. Just fine. Maybe the cottage wouldn't have to be sold after all.

"Ida, we'd better be going back," Brittany said. "We've got some things to do at the cottage, and we plan to drive on into town tonight."

Ida immediately glided over to a cupboard and began rustling out paper sacks and napkins from a drawer. "Not without some honey and biscuits."

"Oh, Ida." Brittany laughed. "Don't trouble—"

"Speak for yourself, Ms. Winters." Sam kissed Missy on top of a thicket of curls and set her gently on the floor. "I for one will drive better by a factor of ten with Ida's biscuits at my side."

Ida beamed.

"And you," he continued to Brittany, "if you behave yourself, can share them with me." He tugged on a loose strand of her hair and let his fingers rub gently against her cheek. "Okay?"

She grinned. "Okay."

Good-byes were hugs for everyone and promises to come back soon, and Brittany finally pulled Sam down the back steps and through the yard to the edge of the woods.

"Okay, Lawrence, 'fess up," she whispered with mock seriousness. "Where did you become so adept at diaper patrol? I'm beginning to think you have a baseball team of children hidden away somewhere that you've forgotten to mention."

"Do you want the truth or an elaborate tale that would add color to the day?"

"Sam, you're about all the color I can handle today. Let's try truth."

"That's fine too." He wound his arm about her shoulders and led her out of a patch of fading sunlight and into the cool dampness of the woods. "Once upon a time, there was a—"

"Sam!"

"Right, truth." He drew his brows together seriously. "I spent some time with some French friends one spring while I did an article for a magazine on photography."

"You *write* too?"

"Shh, my love, you're interrupting my truth." He tapped his fingers lightly on her lips, leaving them tingling. "My friend Simone happened to give birth to twins the second week I was there. Anthony *Samson* Boullier and his sister, Nicole."

"Samson?"

"Uh-huh." He nodded proudly. "He's a handsome, terrific kid, and Nicole is a charmer. Someday you will meet them. Anyway, I was there, and home writing much of the time, so I appointed myself their temporary Uncle *Nounou*."

"Sam . . . " she murmured.

"I *do* like the way you say my name, Ms. Winters." He smiled at her, then added seriously, "I had a *wonderful* time with those babies. Leaving them was one of my more painful farewells. But I see them whenever I can."

"Well," Brittany said, wrapping one arm around him, "I shall tuck that info away in case I should ever need a diaper man."

"You whistle, I'll come," he said quietly, and led her around a thick tree branch that had tumbled over the path.

They walked in silence for a while, their breath white

puffs in the cold air, each sifting through the tangle of emotions that clouded their thoughts. The afternoon sun had melted most of the snow and left the woods full of the clean odor of nutritious mulch beneath their feet. Wet pine needles stuck to the soles of their shoes and a soft shuffle accompanied their slow walk.

"I see why you love it here," Sam said presently. "I'm sorry for you that your father's selling it."

She nodded. "I thought about buying it myself."

"Why don't you?"

She shrugged. "I don't know. It's such a big house, I guess I felt selfish. It's a family house, a house for children, not a place for just me."

"It's the kind of place that could mend spirits, replenish the soul."

She looked up at him, her face still. Why had he said that? How much of her soul could he read?

He rubbed his fingers lightly across her slender shoulder. "Your mother said you spent a lot of time here after your trip to Europe."

It wasn't a question, but Brittany sensed an invitation in his voice, if she wanted to take it. She tipped her head back and looked up into the tangled branches of the trees. "Yes, I moved in here for a while." She smiled. "To mend my spirit and replenish the soul."

"It was that difficult for you, to recover from your . . . relationship in Europe?" Why couldn't he just say it—say "man" or "lover"? But it pained him now to think of her loving someone else, even in the past.

She shook her head. "No, it wasn't that. It was really myself I needed to put together again. I didn't have the same kind of feelings—" She was about to say "as I have for you," but she shied from it now and instead began again. "I was very fond of David. We both wanted the same things from our relationship—fun and excitement. I was young in many ways, Sam. I'd never let myself loose like that before and I really *wanted* to. So I did. I was sad when it ended, but had known from the very beginning that it would end. We—neither of us—wanted marriage then."

"But you mourned the relationship. And it still seems to affect you, Brittany . . ."

She shook her head and tightened her grip around his waist, feeling his strength. "No, Sam, I mourned the baby."

He stopped in the middle of the path and stared at her. The sadness in her eyes confirmed her words.

"He . . . left you pregnant?" The clenching of his teeth was nearly audible in the still woods.

"No," she said softly. "He never knew I was pregnant. I didn't know until just before he left. It wasn't in the plan, you see."

"What the hell—"

The storm she spotted in Sam's eyes frightened her, and she quickly placed her hand on his arm, forestalling his words. "You don't understand, Sam. He wasn't the fathering kind. He—he needed to be off, to experience the world, to lift and land when he wanted to." Like you, she whispered painfully in a silent pocket of her mind.

"That's a damn stupid thing to say, Brittany. 'Fathering kind.' What the hell is that?" Both arms had circled her now and held her still in front of him. His eyes bore into hers. "What did you do about the baby?" he asked harshly.

"I loved him for three months. And then I mourned him when I miscarried." Her voice was hushed.

Sam moaned softly as he crushed her to him. "Oh, my sweet Brittany, I'm so sorry."

Tears slid down her cheeks as she pressed her face into his sweater. "I never told anyone before, Sam."

The stillness of the woods cushioned them as they stood with arms wound tightly around each other. With each passing moment Brittany breathed more freely as the sorrow of her memory and the tight ball of pain began slowly to unravel.

"You should have told someone," Sam said. "That's too much to carry alone."

She nodded. "But it doesn't matter. I have now, Sam."

"Were you alone?"

Her head brushed against his sweater and she didn't mind if he saw the tears that rolled down her cheeks. "Yes, I stayed there until after it happened. And then I came back here to recover. No one ever knew. I couldn't bear people telling me how it was all for the best."

He dropped kisses into her hair and held her tightly. "What a hell of a thing to go through."

She drew away slightly and saw the sad understanding in his eyes. "Yes, it was. But it was my bed, Sam, I made it."

There was no self-pity in her voice, only sorrow. He brushed a strand of hair back from her face.

"You know, Sam, until this moment I think I blamed myself for the miscarriage."

"Brittany, that—"

"I know. It doesn't make sense. But I think I did. Deep down, somewhere in my sorrow. Because I had foolishly made a choice . . . to have that affair . . . and the consequences were ones I never considered, never planned for." She flung out the feelings, wanting to release them into the past.

"But it wasn't your fault." He cradled her in his arms, soothing her.

She shook her head and whispered, "No, it wasn't, Sam, was it?"

"No, my love. It wasn't. And you're going to have other babies, and be the most wonderful mother in the world."

She clung to him for a long time, her spirit lifting until she felt scooped out, released, and her breathing grew deeper, smoother. The sorrow lingered, but the sharing had lifted the burden until she could hold it out in front of her, handle it. And in time, she knew now, she could bury it.

They started walking again, Sam's arm wrapped firmly around her shoulder and hers stretched loosely around his waist. Another link had invisibly stretched itself out and bonded the two of them together, and she wondered at the irony of it all, at the way Sam had fallen into her ordered life, had filled such needs in her, becoming her dear friend . . . her lover. Against all reasonable, rational expectations. They were pieces of a puzzle that shouldn't fit together. Her emotional exhaustion prevented any further thought, and all she could manage was a gentle squeeze where her fingers curled into Sam's waist.

"What's that all about?" he asked.

She shook her head and wiped the dampness from her eyes. "Just the result of wandering thoughts. It has something to do with the peculiar twists of fate."

"You don't like twists much, do you, Brittany?"

"No."

"But sometimes they can be a shot in the arm. Sometimes the unexpected can bring real joy."

"Or real sadness."

He nodded. "Sure, I guess so. Life's kind of a mixture."

They walked slowly over the hunks of extended roots that laced their path until Sam stopped. "Life is like this path, Brittany. Look."

The path split into two from where they stood, one part winding to the left, the other to the right. "Just like in the poem, there's one less traveled, and the other heads back home."

"And that's the one to take."

"The safe, sure path . . . always?"

She nodded.

With warm fingers he cupped her chin and looked deeply into her eyes. "You worry too much, Brittany. Take life more as it comes."

"I tried that once, Sam. I was carefree and spontaneous and free." Her voice dropped. "And it didn't work. At least not for me."

He saw the sorrow slip back into her. "No more sadness for today, my Brittany. We'll deal with it all in its time." His hands held her head back and her lips were ready when he covered them with his own, softly at first, and then with a fiercely tender passion that arose from the center of him.

Finally he pulled back and smiled down at her with desire glazing his eyes. "But this once—just this once, mind you—you're right about the short path. Because if we don't take it, I'm going to have to lay you down in the snow right here, and who knows what the squirrels and bunnies will think?"

"They might think we're taking a chance," she said with all the lightness she could muster, and clung to his hand tightly as he pulled her through the darkening shadows of dusk toward the cottage.

"I don't want to go back, ever." Brittany slid her head into the tight stretch of denim that was Sam's lap and watched the fire dancing brightly in his eyes. She felt ecstatically spent and wanted to savor the feeling forever.

"I'm all for it." he murmured, his fingers blazing hot trails across her face and down her neck. She wore nothing but an oversized shirt she'd pulled from a closet when she got up to make coffee, and Sam wondered if it were possible for anyone to look lovelier. He didn't think so.

"Sam." Her eyes grew wistful and she rubbed her cheek against the smooth nakedness of his stomach. "I don't think I've ever felt this way before. So . . . so completely full."

"I was thinking the same thing."

"Does it frighten you?"

Her question surprised him. It *did* frighten him, he realized, but not in the way she meant. What frightened him wasn't the incredible feeling of love, or the warmth that flooded through him when he looked at her, or the desire that overwhelmed him at the most unexpected moments. These things were what dreams were made of, and far too precious to be tarnished by fear.

But what frightened the bejesus out of him was what would come next.

The thought of living without Brittany wasn't an option. She'd become the stuff of his life, whatever it was that made his heart beat and his soul soar.

The thought of marriage caused a tightening in his throat that he couldn't explain to anyone; he felt it might possibly choke every breath of life out of him. And then what good would he be to Brittany? He'd be a nothing, able to give her nothing, and she deserved so very much. Thoughts of the baby she'd lost flooded his mind, and he felt a stinging sensation behind his eyes. He clenched his jaw.

"Sam? What's wrong?" Brittany saw the shadows darken his face. He suddenly looked so sad that she wanted to cradle him in her arms and assure him it would be all right, that they could vanquish whatever it was that was pulling him away from her into a private pain.

"Nothing, my love. Come here." He slid his hands beneath her head and lifted her up. The hot press of her lips made his worry slip away. "Ahh, that's better."

She nipped lightly at his bottom lip. "Better than what?"

"Mmm . . ." He brushed her moist, parted lips. "Better than just about anything."

She dug her hands into his hair, clinging to him, knowing exactly what he meant.

Ten

"I'd say you're looser these days, Brittany, and that pleases me immensely." Frances Sullivan patted away a wrinkle from her handsome wool dress. "It's good for you, you know."

Brittany pushed the rabbit cage over to the side of the lounge and straightened. "Loose?" she wondered. Brittany Winters, a loose woman? Hmmmm, well, she could live with that. She swallowed a smile and looked back at the stately woman. "So 'being loose' is good for me, Miss Sullivan? Last week it was laughing."

"Yes, certainly, and it's true you know. Does wonderful things for the chemical balance in your body. Norman Cousins helped cure an illness by laughing. And you are laughing more, yes."

"Will it cure my illness?" Brittany mused, half aloud.

"It will help considerably, dear. And your illness happens to be one we should all suffer from." With the gentle care she afforded her Lalique sculptures, she picked up the rabbit named Delilah and glided grandly across the room.

Brittany watched her leave with a bemused smile.

"She's right for once."

Brittany spun around. It was Eustelle Cleaver, leaning on her cane and waiting for Piggy to bring back the ball she'd rolled across the floor. "Mrs. Cleaver, good morning! I see you have a new cane."

"No, I don't think it will rain. But even if it did, your nice smile, Brittany, would be all the sunshine we'd need around here. It's good for you, you know."

Brittany lifted one eyebrow, and said loudly, "So I hear. Why do I get the feeling, Mrs. Cleaver, that there's a conspiracy regarding my health around here?"

The remark tickled Mrs. Cleaver, and her laughter tinkled like wind chimes. "Oh, you. It's your *mental* health, we care about. You know"— she thumped one hand against her breast—"affairs of the . . ."

Brittany shook her head and laughed lightly. "Well, it's nice to know there's all this concern about me."

"What's the matter with your knee?" Mrs. Cleaver's thin brows lifted in concern.

Brittany smiled gently and slipped her a dog biscuit to give to Piggy. "My knee's just fine, thanks, Mrs. Cle—"

"And where *is* he, anyway?" cut in Mr. Aldrich, who, ever since the dance, seemed to be trailing close behind Eustelle.

"Piggy?" Brittany asked.

"No, Sam, Sam. You know."

"Oh, *him*." She smiled. "Do you need him for something?"

"I need some books he promised me, and we need some more scripts for the playreading group. And he owes me a checker game."

"Oh, I see. Well, I'll tell him. He's been working hard on finishing a game, but I'm sure he'll drop those by if he said he would."

"Yep, Sam's a man of his word. Do y'suppose he'll keep on coming by here, though, when the game's finished?" He laughed and Brittany noticed his hand creep up and rest on Mrs. Cleaver's shoulder. "That was his excuse, y'know—to get information from you."

Brittany nibbled on her lower lip as she fished through

her mind for an answer. It was the kind of question she'd been avoiding zealously. What *did* happen when the game was finished next week? In the two weeks since the weekend at the cabin, she and Sam had both avoided the topic like the plague. She couldn't face it, not yet. Shaking her head, she smiled. "I'm sure he'll be back, Mr. Aldrich. If only to play that checker game." Quickly she made her exit, slipping out into the hall to find the program director and force herself to deal with things she could control.

She spotted the tall, friendly redhead standing behind the reception desk and quickly walked over to her.

"How does this look to you, Sheila?" she asked, handing her the clipboard with the coming week's schedule attached.

Sheila read through it quickly. "Looks great, Brittany. I've one favor, though . . ."

"Oh?"

"You know that playreading group Sam organized?"

Brittany nodded, smiling. "The one that likes to meet on a dance floor?"

Sheila nodded, and she and Brittany both glanced down the hall as loud hammering from the social hall broke into their conversation.

"Whatever they're working on now certainly is noisy!" Brittany said.

Sheila only smiled mysteriously. "Right. Well, turns out they're reading everything they can get their hands on, not just plays, and they've scheduled a 'public' performance. Any chance you and Sam could make an extra trip out here for it? Sam knows about it, but we hadn't set the date when he was here last week."

Before Brittany could answer, Sheila went on, intent on getting all her reasons in. "Now, I know Sam's busy putting the finishing touches on your father's game, but I also know he wants to be here for it. And it'd mean so much to the folks if you both could come."

"Of course I can come, Sheila. I'd love to! I can't speak for Sam, but . . ." Her voice trailed off. No, that wasn't entirely true. She *could* speak for Sam, easily. Since the weekend up in the woods they'd been together every spare minute, and when they couldn't be together, they were wishing they were. And when they weren't wishing, Sam was calling her on the phone and whispering things to her that turned her bones to mush and ignited forest fires deep in her belly.

"Actually, I guess I *could* speak for Sam," she said slowly. "After all, he is the founding father of this. He should be here."

"Yes, he needs to be here."

"Well, I'll make sure he is. Don't worry, Sheila. I'll have him here in the front row."

"Sirius is winking at you," Sam said, pointing at the wintry sky as he and Brittany walked up the winding drive to the Elms Home a few days later. "Fitting."

"We understand each other, Sirius and me." She linked her arm through Sam's and pressed closely to his side, her head tilted back to the starry sky. "I almost named Dunkin Sirius, you know."

"But?" Sam looked down into her eyes and could see the flickering lights of the stars in them.

"Well, Dunkin was orphaned, you see. And we found him—"

"Let me guess. He was found on the steps of a doughnut store."

Brittany beamed. "Exactly. Sam, *we* understand each other." She kissed him lightly on the cheek.

"Well, since we're talking serious . . ."

She groaned and burrowed her head into his shoulder.

"*And* since we understand each other so well, there's a serious problem I'd like to discuss with you."

Her smile faded until she looked up and saw the

teasing laughter in his eyes. "I see. . . . Well, yes, sir, Mr. Lawrence. What can I do to help?"

"Everything! You see, there's this woman I'm crazy about, and for the past few days I've been working like a madman to finish a game job—for *her* father, in fact."

She scratched her chin and deepened her voice in mock seriousness. "Yes, yes, go on."

"And well, you see, we haven't seen each other much for these few days, a phone call here and there, maybe—"

"Maybe?" Her brows shot up. "Here and there?"

"Well, actually there were a number of phone calls made, at odd hours occasionally. But they were necessary, you see . . ."

"Of course."

"But phone calls don't quite do the trick."

"Trick?" She gasped. His hand had slipped beneath the opening in her coat and moved slowly to capture one full breast that was covered tantalizingly by a soft cashmere sweater.

"Yeah." His voice deepened with the circling pressure he applied to her breast. "The problem won't go away. I need help." He pulled her into the shadow of a huge maple tree.

"Help . . ." Her breath was coming in short, tiny gasps now as she wound her arms around his neck and held on for dear life. Any strength she had ever had in her legs was gone, turned to putty as his mouth covered hers in hot, hungry kisses.

"Uh-huh." He finally allowed a minute slice of space between them. "Seems this woman has cast a spell on me."

"And?" She breathed the single word with difficulty.

"And I'm horny as hell!"

His outburst snapped the spell between them and she threw back her head and laughed into the cold wintry air. "Oh, Sam. You do have a way with words."

He slapped his head and groaned. "I'm in terrible, body-racking pain, and the lady laughs!"

She wound one arm around his waist and hugged him tightly. "Sam, Sam—"

"The lecherous man," he finished, breathing heavily into her hair.

"Not ever." She looked up, her love for him shining in her eyes. "Now, come on, lover boy, calm yourself down. The curtain goes up in ten minutes and I *promised* to have you there."

"Well, I hope the lights stay out," he mumbled as he followed her up the stairs and through the wide front door. "My body can't stand too much scrutiny tonight."

She just shook her head and grinned, trying to calm her own fires that licked teasingly within her.

The halls were empty and they hurried around the corner to the social hall, where they were greeted warmly by Sheila.

"I think the show is about to begin," Sheila said. "There are two seats right there on the aisle." She pointed over several rows of heads.

Sam and Brittany nodded and made their way down the makeshift aisle, waving at the people who smiled up at them.

"Look, Sam, there's Billy." Brittany pointed down toward the front, where Bertha Hussey sat proudly between her grandson and his new girlfriend.

Two weeks ago Bertha had mentioned to Sam that she was worried about Billy, who had been having problems finding a job. A few days later Sam had hired him to take care of the plants in his office.

"He's done great things with my plants," Sam whispered proudly to Brittany. "I'd swear they're multiplying daily! The gang has promised me they'll keep him on permanently."

Brittany's head jerked up. "What—what do you mean?" Her voice was so soft Sam didn't seem to hear her, and instead of answering he ushered her toward the empty seats.

"Lights are blinking, Brittany. We'd better sit down."

Her heart was pounding in her ears. What did he mean *they* would keep Billy on? Why not him? Where would *he* be? His talk of moving on had become something she purposely paid little attention to. After all, he never elaborated, and had always made it sound so indefinite. Besides, in her world people settled down at Sam's age, didn't "move on" to other ventures, other cities, other *countries*, for Lord's sake! The thoughts were jumbled in her head and she breathed deeply, willing them away. She'd probably heard him wrong anyway. She pushed a smile back into place and looked up toward the front of the room.

A half-dozen sheets had been carefully sewn together and threaded on a wire so that they fell in soft folds, separating the audience from the forward part of the social hall. In front of the sheet was a podium and a microphone. "Do you know anything about this?" she whispered to Sam.

He gave her a secret smile and squeezed her leg playfully, then let his fingers rest lightly on her thigh.

"Is that a yes or a no?" She played fire with fire and returned the caress until she saw Sam's jaw quiver.

"Brittany Ellsbeth, I'm not going to be responsible for my actions if you continue to molest me in this manner," he muttered between his teeth.

"I'll take full responsibility, Mr. Lawrence. Now, confess to me, what's going on here tonight?"

"*You* brought *me*, remember?" He slid his hand beneath hers and separated her fingers, twining his own between them until their palms were flat together. "I did help dig up some skits for them and threw out a few ideas here and there, but I haven't seen it all together. Satisfied?" He bent over and kissed the end of her nose.

She nodded, wanting to kiss him back in a manner totally unbefitting the opening act of a senior citizens' variety show, but was saved from temptation by the resonant sounds of rolling drums coming from behind the curtain.

The crowd noises dimmed to a soft hush as a slim, elegant figure swept toward the podium from a hidden spot in the shadows. It was Frances Sullivan at her regal best. A long shimmering gown covered her graceful frame and it sparkled in the lone spotlight that lit her face. She reached for the microphone and greeted the eager audience.

"Good evening, friends and relatives," she began, her eyes and smile rippling over the rows of people.

She paused when she came to Sam, or so it seemed to Brittany and her poised smile broadened just a tiny bit before she went on.

"I think Frances likes you," she whispered to Sam.

He held her hand tightly in his and moved it slowly back and forth across his thigh. "I think Frances knows you're doing crazy things to me back here."

"Sam!"

"Shh." He gestured to Frances. "You'll miss something."

Frances's golden voice continued from the far end of the room. "We have a wonderful surprise for you all tonight. Why, some of our own residents don't even know about this yet.

"Due to the kind generosity of a dear friend, and the unstinting efforts and wonderful talents of some of our residents, we are unveiling tonight an addition to our Elms Home that will bring hours of joy into all our lives."

"That's what you do for me, you know," Sam whispered into her hair. "Hours and hours of joy."

Her eyes were glassy but stayed glued to Frances.

"If Mr. Fitzgerald will please come out and help me with the cords, the unveiling shall take place."

Dressed in his sedate wedding and funeral suit, and looking as handsome as an Irish rogue, Jerry Fitzgerald gripped the rope that had been tied to the top of one of the center sheets. Frances did the same to the other, then paused just long enough to excite interest in every last soul in her audience. Then she nodded her head slightly, and she and Jerry walked in opposite directions, slowly pulling open the curtain of sheets.

"Oh, my," Brittany whispered, as first a hush, and then a chorus of excited ohs and ahs filled the room.

Beyond the sheets a permanent theater stage filled the entire end of the room, complete with a cranberry velvet curtain that fell in soft rippling folds to the stripped hardwood floor, and rows of lights positioned high on the new stage ceiling. There was a small orchestra pit, an apron on either side of the stage with steps on one and a short ramp on the other that led down into the "theater," and built-in microphones in strategic locations.

"Sam, isn't it wonderful?" She looked over at him, but even before their eyes met, a rush of understanding flooded over her. "Oh, Sam . . . you . . ."

"Nice, isn't it?"

She laid her hand against his cheek. "Not nearly as nice as the 'dear friend' who made it possible."

"What do you know about anything?" He leaned close and brushed a kiss across her lips. "Now, let's keep our fingers crossed that it all works."

To the sound of another drum roll, The Elms Home First Annual Variety Show began in earnest. The curtain swept back and Joseph Aldrich shuffled out onto center stage in an oversized white coat and regaled the audience with a rendition of the doctor scene from *The Sunshine Boys*. A lovely young blond volunteer filled in as the voluptuous, buxom nurse and Mr. Aldrich played the scene to the hilt, bulging his eyes at the sight of her straining bosom, and pushing his audience to the edge of their seats with laughter when he stumbled and his large nose wedged directly into her deep shadowy cleavage.

Sam laughed uproariously and beside him Brittany

wiped tears of delight from her eyes. Everyone in the room was laughing, and as she looked around her, she saw so many old faces lit with new life.

The mood switched quickly to a more controlled enjoyment as Frances Sullivan introduced the next act, a brief excerpt from *Our Town*. "Why, that's Bertha Hussey," Brittany whispered in amazement. The shy, quiet lady was perched on a tall stool, her hair brushed to a glossy sheen, and her voice resonant with near-Shakespearean thunder as she read through her lines.

"Look at Billy," Sam said.

Billy was sitting on the edge of his seat, his hand holding his girlfriend's, and fat tears were rolling down his face as he watched his grandmother's moment of glory.

"Oh, Sam." Brittany blinked back a tear.

Sam's arm slipped over the back of her chair and held her close.

Our Town was followed by several short but loud numbers from the Bronze Boys Brass Band, followed by a barber shop quartet, and then the finale.

The lights dimmed, then rose again, this time painting the stage in all the brilliant colors of an English garden and spotlighting a grouping of white wicker furniture and three elegant Elms Home women. They sat with their parasols in place, and their voices were full of a lifetime of loving as they thoughtfully, dramatically, recited a litany of poems that celebrated life.

The room was so still that the slightest rustle of the women's graceful gowns were heard, as were the tiny breaks in their old voices that spoke with unbearable honesty of living and loving and dying.

Frail Betta Hopper's voice quivered like a bird's as she recited the words of Rupert Brooke. And Frances Sullivan's melodious voice spoke of strawberries on summer afternoons in the Kilpatrick hills with a loved one as they laughed with life and love.

And old Mrs. Cleaver, her knotted hands cupped beneath a trembling chin, left not a dry eye in the house as she sifted through her memories and shared her days of joy, and her life's pallet of color.

The crowd was still as the brand new velvet curtain danced shut across the stage. The spell was broken when the lights went on, and the audience rose to its feet en masse. They cheered the variety show troupe with ringing applause until finally Frances Sullivan swept back onto the stage and announced that punch and pastries would be served in the lounge momentarily.

Brittany wrapped her arms around Sam and hugged him tightly. "Oh, Sam, it was *wonderful*!" She tipped her chin up and their eyes met. "You should have told me, I could have donated."

His head moved from side to side. "No, love, this one was mine. They've been so terrific to me, and the money wasn't a problem. I *wanted* to do it. The idea came so naturally that Frances and I wondered why it had taken so long for me to think of it."

"You're wonderful. And I love you so very much."

He wove his fingers through the fine curls at the back of her neck and pressed his lips to her cheek. "Any chance we could skip the punch and pastries?" he whispered huskily.

Her head moved against his lips. "No, but we can certainly eat fast."

They were separated at the reception by the crush of people wanting to tell Sam how wonderful his gift of a theater was, and it wasn't until he slipped his arm around Brittany's waist and pulled her into the shadows of a deserted hallway an hour later that they were able to make their escape.

The trip back to her house was silent, filled with an urgency that electrified the air in Sam's small car.

"Brittany, we should talk." His hand slid over and up onto her lap.

"No, Sam, not just yet," she whispered, lifting his fingers to her lips and kissing them gently. She needed to love him desperately, right now! Before talk crept in and robbed her of her happiness. Her mind flashed crazily with images, Sam leaning on the fireplace mantel in her parents' home . . . Sam and Miss Sullivan waltzing across the floor . . . Sam with tiny Missy Plunkett balanced on his knees . . .

And Sam, *her* Sam, holding her, loving her, making her whole again.

The engine died in front of the carriage house just in time for her to blink back her tears and flee up the steps with Sam a shadow at her back.

"Brittany, honey, you're way ahead of me," he said, breathing heavily as they slipped through the door. "I know there's a fire burning inside of me, but is there another one I don't know about?"

She snapped the door shut behind him, then turned slowly and wrapped her arms around his neck. "There's one right here, Sam, right inside me," she whispered. "Shall we match flame for flame?"

Sam's body was already alive, and when he saw the love and desire that brimmed in her eyes, his heart swelled.

His mouth came down forcefully on hers, his lips grinding against hers until they parted and welcomed the greedy exploration of his tongue. His kiss was hot and fierce and she responded with an intensity that stunned him.

"Oh, Brittany," he moaned, running his fingers through her hair. "You're making me crazy. But do you . . . suppose . . . we could take off our coats?"

Wordlessly, she let her heavy coat fall to the floor, her eyes never leaving his face. While he shrugged out of his and dropped it onto the chair beside the door, she kissed him again, then slowly unhooked the pearl buttons running down the front of her dress. She stepped out of the dress, then took Sam's hand and lifted his fingers to the lacy camisole that barely covered her quivering breasts.

"Love me," she said simply.

"Oh, sweetheart." His words were labored. "I thought you'd never ask." He bent his head until his lips found the damp skin beneath the wisp of lace, and he dropped tiny kisses along the rise of her breasts.

Her head fell back and she whimpered with longing, feeling the moist rush of desire flood her. Nothing mattered tonight, nothing in the whole world but joining herself with Sam and loving him with a fervor she couldn't seem to control. "Come, Sam." She shuddered, and managed to clasp his hand and pull him urgently through the darkened living room and into the bedroom, lit softly by a single shaft of the moon streaming through the window.

She leaned against the brass bedpost in her lace briefs and camisole as she waited for him to slip out of his clothes.

He piled them in a heap and turned toward her, then stopped abruptly, rooted to the spot, his breath tight in his throat. For as long as he'd live he knew he'd never forget the vision of Brittany at that moment, her lips swollen and moist from his kisses, her breasts straining against the silky material, and her gold-flecked eyes loving him completely. Slowly he walked toward her.

"I love you, Brittany. I love you so much." He framed her face with his hands, holding it still. "So very, very much."

He kissed away the tear that escaped her eye and fell slowly from the golden lash, then slid his hands down her arms. "Here, we don't need this." With sure fingers he lifted the delicate lace camisole and peeled it away, then pressed his hands inside the silky panties and slid them easily down her legs. "Now we're equal," he whispered into the darkness.

She answered with a feathery touch, her fingers running lightly over his chest and circling each nipple slowly. Lowering her head, she licked each light brown point, nipping and sucking until Sam's groan of desire filled the still room.

Embracing her, he slid his hands down her back until they cupped the warm flesh of her buttocks and pressed her forward.

"Oh, Sam," she said breathlessly as her breasts were crushed against his chest and the full strength of his arousal pressed hotly against her. She knotted her hands in his hair, clinging to him as he moved slowly until her body throbbed painfully with desire.

"Oh, Sam, please, I need you so . . ."

Gently he lifted her onto the high bed, his fingers sure and solid beneath her, holding her to him, moving her hips until her legs slid apart and he pressed forward, entering her.

She sighed. Then the sound was cut off as he began to thrust slowly in and out, and she could feel the pulsing of his blood within her. When her breathing became labored, she dug her fingers deeply into his shoulders, and then nothing was left but the weightless sensation of soaring off into the universe with Sam. She and Sam and a thousand stars. A rush of pure joy filled her, then exploded into the sky as she filled the air with a great gut-springing cry of love.

The harsh glare of morning light woke Brittany hours later and she knew, even before Dunkin proudly sported the note tied to his collar, that Sam wasn't there. But he'd left her with the afterglow of his loving that lifted a smile to her face and filled her with a warmth that warded off all traces of the chilly morning air.

"Thank you, Dunkin." She tousled the dog's silky head and untied the note, then read slowly:

My love,

Your face speaks of dreams I don't dare disturb, so I'm going to kiss you gently and go off to meet the printer.

It's our final run—and the game will be finished, ready for the grand retirement gala on Friday.

You've brought me more happiness than a lifetime deserves—

My love,
Sam

Eleven

"Checkmate!" Dr. Frank threw his hands in the air, then slapped Sam jovially on the back. "Finally! And I'm not going to let the fact that you look like hell diminish my victory one tad." He looked over his glasses at Sam. "What's bothering you, Sam? Your look sure doesn't match that of the princess. Do you know something she doesn't?"

"Oh, it's just a cluttered mind, Doc. For a guy who sometimes makes his living solving puzzles, I'm not doing so well right now."

Dr. Frank leaned back in the chair and stroked his chin. "Other people's problems I'm good at. Shoot, Sam, maybe I can help."

Sam shook his head. "Thanks, Frank, but I'm not sure anyone can help. You see . . ." He reached across the table and lifted his pipe from the ashtray. There was an unusually perplexed look in his eyes as he gazed at Dr. Frank. "I happen to be hopelessly, head over heels—in love."

Frank nodded. "Okay, Sam, so what else is new?"

"Frank, it's serious. I love her." He sucked in a deep breath and closed his eyes. "But I'm the wrong man for her, and I'm not quite sure what to do about it."

"Hmmmm, that *is* a problem," Frank said slowly. "Does Brittany know you're the wrong man for her?"

Sam shrugged. "I think we've both been too happy with each other to tangle with the facts."

"Perhaps you could tangle with those facts together? Give each other a little more time? Maybe you can't see the forest for the trees, Samson my friend."

Sam smiled at Dr. Frank and pulled himself from the chair at the sound of Brittany's van pulling into the driveway. "Maybe. I've kind of been thinking along those same lines. But right now the person I need to see is Britt—"

"Sam!" She swept into the office like a March wind, throwing her arms tightly around Sam. She grinned a hello at Dr. Frank, who patted her on the shoulder as he exited from the room, then directed her full attention to the man she was still holding in her arms. "I thought you would have called yesterday."

"You got Dunkin's note?"

She lowered her head and blushed. "Of course. But that was a whole day ago."

"I needed to fight battles at work, get all the last minute printing snafus ironed out for the game. But it's all coming together. Everything will be ready for the great presentation Friday night."

"And you'll be there, Sam."

"Well, your mother seems to think I should be. She won't accept the fact that I'm hired help."

Brittany half-smiled. There was more Sam wanted to say. . . .

"Brittany, we need to go somewhere and talk. Right now."

"I'm scheduled—"

"Have Dr. Frank's assistant do it." His voice was urgent. "Please, Brittany."

She searched his eyes. So this was it, she thought, the time for "talk." "I guess we do need to talk, Sam."

Her voice was teasing, low-pitched. "But frankly, I'm not sure why. We communicate so well without words."

He laughed huskily. "Watch it, little lady. You know what that tone of voice does to me." He began nudging her through the reception room and toward the door, then called back over his shoulder, "She'll be back, Doc. Sometime."

"Fine, fine, take all the time you need," Frank mumbled from the lab, pleased as punch that someone was finally taking his advice on something.

Brittany shivered as the wintry wind fanned the chill already creeping through her. "Well, Sam, where to?"

"I don't know, anywhere." He opened the door to his car and held it for her to get in, then hurried around to the other side.

"Brittany, I—" He stretched his arm out and drew her to him until she was tight in his arms, her head nuzzled against his cheek and the clean smell of her filling his senses. "Oh, my, how I do love you," he murmured into her hair.

"I love you too, Sam," she said softly, wishing that was all that mattered, but knowing in her heart this was just the beginning of the conversation.

"I wandered around like a crazy man last night, trying to figure this whole damn thing out. It doesn't make any sense."

She slid her hands to his chest and looked up into the eyes that looked into her soul the way no man had ever before. She shook her head slowly. "I know what I've been doing, Sam. I've been buying time with you."

"No, Brittany." His fingers played with the hair at the back of her neck.

"Shh, Sam, let me at least have my say. I knew from the very beginning what you were all about. You *told* me, remember?" She smiled sadly. "And you knew what you were dealing with also. You know my fears, my dreams. You know I want children, a regular life."

"Sure, Brittany, we both knew that, and in spite of it

we fell in love. You've brought a life to me I never imagined possible, a totally unfamiliar joy that I don't seem to be able to get enough of."

Then don't leave me, Sam, she begged silently. *Marry me.* But she didn't speak aloud. She only listened, and watched. She knew he meant every word of what he was saying. He did love her, with a power and intensity that filled her to the brim. And in spite of all the facts, what they knew about each other, for weeks now she'd nursed a secret hope that this love would somehow solve their differences.

"I've always known what I was about, Brittany, until you. You've shaken it all." He tipped her chin back until she had to look into his eyes. "I haven't been able to solve this puzzle yet, but one thing I know for sure, I'm not ready to give you up."

She fought the tears that stung beneath her lids and tried to keep her gaze steady.

"Brittany, I'd like you to move in with me." His eyes spoke of his love, but all she could feel was the pain of his words as they slowly sank into her consciousness.

"To move—" she began.

He kissed the top of her head and rushed on. "I know, I know, it's not the ideal solution, but until we can figure this all out, please, Brittany, we need more time."

She swallowed hard and bit down on her lower lip to stop it from quivering. "Sam . . ."

"I know it's not careful and planned and secure, I know it's a risk, but *please* think about it—until we can figure this out."

"I can't, Sam, I can't do that." Her voice was harsh and each ragged edge cut through her heart. How could he ask her this? He *knew*—

"Brittany, darling, I know what you've been through. But you and I are different."

Different? she thought. How different could this be? How could she have given her heart to a man who was so afraid to make a commitment? She felt the earth beginning to shake beneath her and her love contorted into a painful, searing sorrow.

"Brittany." Sam held her shoulders and spoke slowly, willing her to listen. "Sometimes you need to risk a little in order to gain in the end. Please, don't turn away. Listen to me."

She swallowed around the lump in her throat and lifted her head slowly. "Sam, I can't. I can't chance it. I can't do it. Without commitment all that's *left* is risk . . . and I can't base my life on that. I can't." Her voice broke as the tears began to flow unchecked down her cheeks.

He tried to say more but she couldn't hear it, not now while the pain was so choking. She fumbled for the door handle and slipped outside. Only at the last second did she look back.

Sam was sitting motionless in the car, his head lowered, his knuckles white on the steering wheel. But there weren't any words left, and she turned and walked slowly back to the clinic.

Brittany hung up the phone, then frowned at it.

Please don't ring again, she told it silently. That ringing made her think of Sam, and she would hear his voice in her mind and her heart would shatter into a million pieces all over again. So, Mother, and Sara and Gordie, she continued, don't call to chat, or talk about the plans for Dad's retirement dinner. Her life had fallen apart and she didn't give a damn about menus and guest lists and whether to wear wool or winter silk.

With great care she picked up the narrow-necked watering can with the sprinkle of painted flowers circling it and slowly soaked the soil of each plant in the sun-drenched living room. Pulling her brows into a frown, she snapped unsightly yellow leaves off one plant and stuffed them into the pocket of her jeans, then removed a layer of dust from another plant with the damp pad of her finger, rubbing the green oval to a waxy shine. Dunkin padded after her, his large eyes curious.

There, she thought. Now she'd move those small begonias to the south windows for the winter, and that'll be finished. She smiled, greatly pleased with the care she had given her plants, then slipped down quietly into the oak rocking chair near the fireplace, folded her knees up beneath her chin, and sobbed.

They were wrenching cries that came from the very deepest part of her and shook her body. Tears streamed down her cheeks and collected in tiny puddles on the folds of her jeans. Why had she let this happen? How could she go through life like this, carrying this ponderous love within her? But she would, she knew. She'd bounce back somehow. She'd carry on and work at the Elms and help Dr. Frank. But she would never, ever love like this again.

Dunkin sat down in front of her and lapped his tongue affectionately across her bare feet. Then, feeling as hopeless as his mistress, he hunched his body down and stuck his head beneath his furry paws.

She groped on the side table for the tissue box, but knew before she hit the cardboard that it was empty.

Painfully, she lifted her head. "Okay, Brittany Ellsbeth, this is it. Pull yourself together. There's no more tissues, what choice do you have but to face the world?" Face the world . . . without Sam . . . The tears swelled again, but this time she held them in check, dragged herself up from the chair, and marched into the bedroom to get ready for work.

These three days without Sam had been the most excruciating experience she had ever been through, and she knew one thing for certain—it couldn't possibly get any worse. That thought was the only thing that pushed life back into her and forced her to ready herself for Windemere's business-social event of the year: Gordon Winters's retirement gala.

Concerned with Brittany's lack of interest in the party, Katherine Winters had taken matters into her own hands and the day of the party she sent over by special delivery a new gown from Saks.

Brittany pulled it carefully from the layers of tissues and smiled sadly. Mother had magnificent taste. She held the soft black jersey dress up in front of her and looked into the mirror. It would do just fine. One less thing to think about. And that left . . . Sam.

Four days and four nights now, and the crushing pain wasn't any better. And tonight she would see him. But for her father's sake, they'd both smile and greet each other, and for the evening she'd swallow her tears and glide across the dance floor, shift food around on a fine china plate, and hide the sorrow that licked through her savagely.

The dress was a perfect fit and fell with grace over her slender hips. With a dusting of bronze shadow across her lids and a light touch of lipstick, she knew she was as ready as she'd ever be for the night ahead.

The dinner was held in the elegant clubhouse of the Windemere Yacht Club, and Brittany gazed in awe at the lines of chauffeured limos stretching along the gas-lit drive. She'd driven over with Dr. Frank, and the two laughed at the scene.

"Must have hired them in from Bridgeport," Dr. Frank joked as he took Brittany's arm, guiding her up the slate walkway to the wide wooden doors.

"You know, Doc, you look mighty handsome in your tuxedo. I fear I'll have to fight for your affections tonight." She squeezed his arm warmly.

"Hah! Not when I have the most beautiful girl in the world on my arm tonight." He looked down at her. "And don't get me wrong, Brittany. I appreciate you more than anyone on God's green earth, but the truth is you shouldn't be hanging on an old codger's arm tonight. You should be—"

"There's nothing old about you, Dr. Frank," she said softly. "And whatever you were going to say next, please don't."

He stared at her intently, but merely said, "Okay, sweetie. You know what I think though?"

"Dr. Frank, I *do* know what you think. And I appreciate it, and love you for it. But— Oh, look, there's Mother." She nodded to a group of elegantly dressed couples being greeted just inside the door by the official hostess for the evening. "I need to say hello."

Frank nodded, took her wool cape, and lumbered off to the checkroom.

Katherine Winters was glorious in a mahogany silk gown that enclosed her tiny frame and set off her sparkling clear eyes like jewels. Brittany hugged her tightly. "You look beautiful, Mother."

"Your father is the one, Brittany dear. Look at him over there. This is quite the most wonderful thing. And darling, Sam brought the game by for me to see ahead—"

Brittany's heart careened at the mention of his name, but her mother seemed not to notice.

"—and it is without a doubt the most clever, beautiful gift imaginable. Your father will be so touched." She gazed lovingly at her husband. "Now, when Sam arrives, make sure he feels at home, dear. He didn't look well today when I saw him, but he promised me he would be here."

Brittany could only nod as her mother swept away to greet new guests. She escaped to her father's side and kissed him on his freshly shaved cheek, finding a childish solace in the familiar scent of his aftershave. "What a dashing guest of honor you make, my handsome father."

Gordon Winters hugged her warmly, then held her away from him and studied her with loving eyes. His gray brows drew together in a frown.

"Brittany, what's wrong?" She should have known this would happen, she thought. Her father never missed anything, not a frown, or a glimmer in her eye, or a secret held in her soul.

"Nothing, Dad. I've been working hard, that's all." She forced a smile to her face. "Come, let me walk with you around the room and feel special." And she led him off into the distraction of the celebration.

Dinner was served later. Toasts were made and crystal glasses clinked together while Brittany sat still, her eyes focused on her parents and her emotions tucked away tightly. She hadn't seen Sam all evening. He must not have come, because even if she didn't see him, she was sure she would feel his presence in the room. Then the chairman of the board rose to the speaker's platform and began his presentation of the grand gift.

Brittany's heart suddenly leaped to her throat. She *could* feel him. He was there in the room somewhere. Slowly she looked up, and without searching the room her gaze fell directly on the man she loved.

He was standing over to the side, beyond the linen-draped dining tables, his tall, lean figure dressed in a handsome tuxedo, his eyes holding hers. Sam had purposely come late. He couldn't bear the thought of watching Brittany all evening and not being able to sweep her up in his arms. Couldn't bear the thought of the pain his love had caused her. She looked beautiful, he thought, and the vulnerability in her eyes only heightened her loveliness. The simple black dress she wore was dramatic and highlighted every beautiful feature, the creamy paleness of her skin. Her gleaming hair was swept off her face in lovely waves that caught the light. Oh, how he ached to touch her, to feel the warmth of her skin. To love her—

He couldn't look away if he had wanted to.

It was only when the chairman spoke his name that the spell was broken and all eyes in the room turned to

Sam. He was being given credit now for the masterful game that was slowly being unveiled at the podium.

Brittany looked over at her father, who was holding up the leather-bound game of his life. Gary's beautiful design had made a masterpiece out of the game board, a sweeping watercolor of Gordon Winters's life to be admired on its own merit. And set in front of Gordon were the gilt-edged game cards that captured the joys and sorrows and private jokes of his life, and the tiny gold playing pieces molded into horses and fishing poles and trophies. The look on her father's face was first one of disbelief, then of thanks, and then, as he began thumbing through the cards, of the tearful joy of memories laid out carefully in front of him. He hugged Katherine tightly to his side, blew a kiss to each of his children sitting proudly along the table, and made a gracious and brief thank-you speech.

"And now, friends," he announced with a sweeping gesture, "please join me in the ballroom to enjoy the truckloads of champagne my lovely wife has ordered, and we'll all have a chance to look more closely at this masterpiece I've been given." His gaze swept over the crowd to where Sam stood. "And I for one can't wait to meet personally the mastermind who has proven once and for all you *can* make a silk purse out of a sow's ear!" The crowd roared festively and within minutes chairs had been shoved back and groups of laughing, happy people moved into the chandeliered ballroom.

Brittany hung back, chatting distractedly to relatives and workers from the plant who had all come to enjoy their beloved boss's special night. "We sure are going to miss him, Miss Winters," she heard again and again. "He's the best there is to work for. The very best."

She could only nod, smiling, trying to keep her thoughts on what they were saying. Then all the excuses to dally walked on into the ballroom and she was left with no choice but to follow.

She spotted Sam immediately. He was standing on the far side of the room with her father. She studied them carefully, the two most important men in her life, side by side. They made a striking portrait, Sam's tawny head next to her father's gently graying one. As she watched, she could see Sam was doing most of the talking, his head bent, her father's still and intent.

"Brittany, may I?" It was Dr. Frank, and she gladly slid into his outstretched arms and glided off on the small dance floor at one end of the room.

"Your father and Sam seem to hit it off mighty nicely," Dr. Frank said carefully.

She nodded.

"But that's no surprise, is it?"

"No," she said slowly. "I guess it's not."

"Is Sam pleased with the way the game turned out?"

"I don't know. We haven't had a chance to speak yet."

The dance ended and Dr. Frank and Brittany smiled at each other while they clapped politely. "Next dance marathon, Brittany, you're mine. I'm claiming you right now." He accepted two glasses of champagne from a passing waiter and handed one to her.

She laughed and took a sip. "You're on, Doc, but I'm not sure I can keep up with you!"

Several others joined them and it was a few minutes before Brittany realized that Sam and her father were talking with a group of people just a short distance behind her. It was her father's voice she heard first.

"A book offer, he tells me, although I can't understand why he wouldn't stay with Creative Games. The company's bound to be a winner."

The group agreed with much enthusiasm, and Brittany listened for the voice she had been waiting to hear.

When it came it was low and friendly. "I know my crew will do a great job without me," Sam said. "Time to move on to something new."

"He's just like you, Gordon," an older man said. "Remember when you were that age? Always shifting that mind of yours from one project to another." He laughed along with the others, then spoke again to Sam. "Tell us about this book, Sam."

"Well, it's for an American publisher, but will involve some time in France . . ."

Brittany felt the blood drain from her face. *France. Sam was doing another book in France . . .* Her thoughts came in spurts now, fragmented and fuzzy, until she had to excuse herself and made her way quickly to the women's lounge. She sank down onto a plush bench and pressed her hands hard against her temples, trying to calm the erratic beating in her head.

It shouldn't upset her like this, she told herself. He had every right to go anywhere he pleased. And hadn't he told her he'd probably turn over the game company to the others? None of this should upset her like this. It shouldn't . . . She felt the tears well up and squeezed her eyes tightly closed to stop the flow.

"Here you are, darling!" Katherine Winters let the door swing closed behind her. "The photographer wants to do a family shot and you're the only one missing."

She started to leave, then slowly turned back to Brittany. "Darling? Are you all right?"

Brittany wet her lips and smiled up at her mother. "I'm fine. I think the emotion of the evening is beginning to get to me."

Her mother bent and kissed her forehead gently. "Yes, perhaps it is." But when Katherine lifted her head there were tiny worry lines around her eyes. She gently clasped Brittany's hand and gazed into her daughter's eyes. "You know, Brittany, I watched your father tonight with such pride and love. But it wasn't always so. Oh, I always loved him, but someone like your father, someone with so many talents and a spirit that won't settle for any kind of cage . . . well, it takes awhile getting used to." She rubbed the back of Brittany's hand absently, her mind seeming to move into the recesses of her memory. "Yes, but it was surely worth it. . . . Her voice drifted off, and when it returned it was full of fresh energy that belied her frail body. "Now come, darling! Let's wipe away that emotion and smile for the cameraman."

Brittany allowed her mother to dab at her face with a wet cloth, then freshened her lipstick and smiled at the image of mother and daughter in the large mirror. Her mother looked different somehow . . . as lovely as always, but something had changed. Or was Brittany looking at her differently, seeing things she'd never noticed before? She slipped her arm around her mother's waist and their eyes met and held in the mirror. "I'm ready now, Mother. Shall we go?"

Somehow Brittany knew even before searching the room that Sam had left. It wasn't his night, and he wouldn't have wanted to take anything away from her father. And although her heart grieved that he hadn't stayed to talk to her, that was all right too. After all, what more was there to say?

Sleep was a restless, relentless tossing, and when Brittany awoke early the next morning, she felt numb and fragmented. Pieces of dreams flitted across her mind and interrupted her thought, and the day seemed icy gray. Her mother's words had strayed into what little sleep there'd been, but Brittany didn't feel ready to deal with what she had said, or even to decide if there was something there to deal *with*. She was so tired. And so alone.

She swallowed too quickly a gulp of steaming coffee and coughed when the heat stung her throat. "Saturday morning, Dunkin. And a million things to do. But what are they?" Her mind wandered off as she grabbed a heavy sweater from the chair and slipped it over her head.

"We'll make a list, Dunkin, like Sam does." Pain bubbled like a lump in her throat and she forced it down. "First, we'll drop those presents of Dad's off at the house. And then I need to talk to Sheila out at the Elms, and then . . ." She searched her mind for the forgotten list, needing desperately to fill every second of the day and block out any chances to think. "Come on, boy, get with it."

The ride to her parents' home was cold, and the old van groaned begrudgingly at each intersection. She rubbed her hands together and blew softly into them. "Winter, Dunkin. It's on its way, mark my words." Dunkin flapped his tail against the seat, then pressed his nose to the window as they pulled into the circle drive of the Winters' estate.

It wasn't until Dunkin's heavy breathing turned into a bark that Brittany noticed another car just pulling away on the other side of the drive. The driver was already past the clump of cedar trees in the center of the drive and couldn't see her unless he had stopped and looked around. He didn't, but it was Sam. Brittany knew it even if it hadn't been for the familiar car or the sandy sweep of hair she glimpsed through the window, or Dunkin's excited bark.

She turned the engine off, then sat still in the van for a minute and tried to collect herself. What was he doing here? And what if she had come a minute sooner? Could she have endured seeing him here? Would she have thrown her arms around him just to feel for an instant the joy of his touch?

She blinked back the tears that leaped into action on a second's notice and forced a cold breath of air into her lungs before swinging her legs out of the van. Dunkin followed in one jump.

"Brittany dear," Katherine called. She was standing on the front step, wrapping her sweater tightly around her. "I thought I heard that vehicle of yours pull up. What a lovely surprise!"

"It's too cold out here, Mother," Brittany said as she walked up the steps," and I can't stay. I just want to unload these gifts from the party last night."

"Oh, yes, dear, how thoughtful." Katherine spun around on her tiny feet and called inside to the butler to unload the van, then turned back and planted a kiss on Brittany's cheek. "It was such a lovely night, wasn't it? Your father was so very pleased."

"Mother, why was Sam here this morning?"

"Sam? Oh, yes, Sam. He came for breakfast."

"Breakfast?" Brittany shoved her hands deep into her pockets and tried to determine what her mother was talking about.

"Yes, dear. He had asked to see your father this morning, so we invited him to breakfast. We do like him so. Then they locked themselves up in the library, just the two of them, until Sam left. It was only minutes after your father left, as a matter of fact. Everyone is so busy this morning."

"Dad left?"

"Yes, Brittany. The—the cottage is sold. And there was some paperwork to take care of."

Brittany shivered and wrapped her arms tightly around her waist. "The cottage . . . I didn't know. About the cottage, I mean. But Ida said there were some interested people."

"Yes, it seems there were." Katherine's smile didn't seem to fit the occasion, Brittany thought, but then her mother hadn't been as attached to the cottage as she had. And yet . . .

She shook her head and stared down at the cement step, her thoughts turning around to Sam again. No, she wouldn't ask any more questions about Sam. She couldn't. Not without breaking her heart wide open right here on the front steps.

"I guess I'd better leave, Mother. I have several stops to make." She kissed her mother on the forehead and sent her back inside before she caught cold. Then she stood there for a long moment, staring out past the driveway as a great shiver passed through her.

Twelve

The Elms Home was quiet when Brittany walked through the front door. This would be her salvation, her peace, she thought. This would help her through.

But deep down inside she knew she'd never be through it completely, because she'd never stop loving Sam as long as she lived.

"Sheila." She spotted the redhead rounding the corner and tried to push a smile into place. "I've brought those field trip plans for you to look over. And the new Petpals schedule."

"Hey, thanks, Brittany. These folks have had such a shot of adrenaline with this theater and all, I think they're ready to tackle just about anything. Old Mr. Fitzgerald's talking about starting a mountain climbing club!"

Brittany smiled. "Can't keep good folks down."

"That's for sure. Those good folks would love to say hello. They missed you this week."

"We had the retirement gala to plan. . . ."

Sheila nodded quickly. "Oh, I understand. But they'd love to say hello if you and Dunkin have the time. There's a group down at the theater."

Brittany glanced down the hall. "It's become a hangout?"

Sheila laughed. "Of sorts. Go on down there. You look like you could use a pick-me-up, and there's no one that can do it to you faster than your friends here."

Brittany nodded and followed Dunkin down the hall.

She turned the corner just in time to hear Bertha Hussey's voice ring out. "Well, I'd make some changes, that I know for sure."

Brittany poked her head inside the room. "Am I interrupting something?"

"Hah!" Mr. Fitzgerald said. "Not you, Brittany. Come on in here and join our little conversation."

She walked to the front of the room, where a small group of residents had collected.

"What's up?" she asked. "Sounds like a serious conversation." She mustered a smile and slipped into one of the chairs.

"Serious and not so serious," Frances said. "We were talking about what we would do over if we had our lives stretched out before us again."

Brittany ran her fingers through her hair and thought of Sam. She'd put him right there, right in the biggest part of her life. And she'd leave him there.

"I know one thing for sure," Mr. Aldrich said in his wheezing voice. "I'd not be so damn afraid of things."

Frances looked at him. "You, afraid, Irving? I wouldn't have thought it."

"Afraid of new things, I mean, Frances. Of trying new things. Fear's a damn shackle, you know. You have only one life, I say, so why not fill it up for all it's worth!"

"Sometimes I think I'd like to be much less serious about things," Frances said. "I'd take more risks, be more risqué . . ."

Bertha giggled into her lace handkerchief.

"But, Frances," Brittany said, "you could have brought sadness into your life by taking all those risks. You have—and have had—a *happy* life."

Frances moved to the chair next to Brittany's and laid one thin hand on top of hers. "All lives have a mixture of both, dear. But sometimes risks will bring enormous happiness, the kind you'd never have a chance for if you weren't willing to dare a little."

Jerry Fitzgerald tapped his cane hard on the floor. "So, folks," he growled in a deep, resonant stage voice, "let's treat life more like an ice cream cone. We'll taste it and love it and eat it up before it melts!"

Tears filled Brittany's eyes and began to spill over.

"And you, young lady," Mr. Aldrich said with gruff affection, "you should laugh more and cry less."

"You're so right," she said, slipping out of her chair. "Thank you all," she added, and hurried up the aisle with Dunkin at her heels.

The tears didn't stop all the way home. Brittany marveled vaguely at that. She hadn't supposed there were that many left in her. She felt drained, but slowly, ever so slowly, the vacuum was being refilled.

Sam Lawrence meant everything in the world to her. And dammit, if he needed more time, she'd give it to him, but she wouldn't be without him in the meanwhile. She *couldn't* live without him. The thought sent a new wave of tears down her cheeks, but she smiled through them. *Oh, Sam, I love you!* She wanted to open the window and shout it along the highway, stand atop a mountain and write it on the wind. But most of all she wanted to whisper it into Sam's ear, again and again and again.

She pulled the van up to the carriage house and ran up the stairs, stopping only long enough to pat Dunkin's head and assure him everything would be all right. "It's got to be all right, Dunkin. It's got to. If he wants to go to France, fine. I'll be there for him when he comes home. I'll show him, Dunkin, it'll be all right.

We belong together, right, boy? And that's worth any risk I need to take."

She shrugged out of her jacket and hung it on the coat rack, then headed for the phone.

Fumbling for the book, she found Sam's number and dialed quickly, then waited. The room was still, except for the wild beating of her heart. She pressed one palm against it and prayed. *Please, Sam, please be there . . .*

After a few minutes she finally hung up. She bit impatiently on her bottom lip, then grinned. The office, of course! He was burying himself in work. She dialed quickly and breathed a sigh of relief when she heard the click on the other end.

"Jill, hello. This is Brittany. May I please speak to Sam?"

"Brittany, hi! Hey, I'm sorry, but he's not here."

Her heart sank all the way down to her tennis shoes. "He's not? Well, have you seen him?"

"Fleetingly. He burst into the office a short while ago, acting kind of strange. Hugged Gary, kissed me on the cheek. Then he made a few phone calls, told us we were wonderful, and then was gone, mumbling something about getting gas for his car and life beginning again. Didn't make much sense to us, Brittany, but you never know with Sam."

"No, I guess not. . . ." Her voice drifted off and she replaced the receiver, her mind spinning. *Oh, Sam, where are you? I need you, my darling. How can I take a risk if the riskee disappears?*

By eight o'clock that evening, Brittany was exhausted. Her calls to Sam had dwindled down to three or four an hour, and with each unanswered call her heart turned over and she felt the same wrenching disappointment. She picked at a cold plate of shrimp her mother had sent over along with other party leftovers, but there wasn't room inside her for anything. Thoughts of Sam consumed her. He was all she needed.

Finally, hours later, she fell across her bed and dropped almost instantly into a deep, dreamless sleep.

Dunkin awoke first, nuzzling the hand that fell limply over the side of the bed.

Brittany pried one eye open, then shut it quickly against the bright, dazzling sunshine that flooded her room. She was still in jeans and a sweater, and she felt awful.

Sam . . . She hadn't found Sam. Suddenly wide awake, she bounded out of bed and headed for the shower. Well, she would today. No matter where he was, she would find him and go to him, and tell him how very much she loved him.

The hot water pelted over her naked body, tingling her flesh, and she smiled up into the spray. Today was a new day. She wouldn't think about yesterday or tomorrow . . . only about today.

When Sam still hadn't answered his phone by noon, Brittany finally called her father. She'd lived alone for too long to drag her parents into her problems, but maybe her father would have some idea where Sam was.

Gordon Winters's deep voice was slow and thoughtful as he pondered her question. "Well, Brittany, haven't you talked to him?"

"No, Dad. And I need to. It's important. And Mother said he stopped by the house yesterday."

There was the trace of a smile in her father's voice when he answered. "Well, yes, he did stop by. We . . . ah, had some business to attend to. But he's not here now."

Of course he wasn't there! she thought, frustrated. "No, I know that, Dad, but I thought you might have some idea where he is, or if he's on a trip. Did he mention anything like that? No one answers at his apartment."

"Well, Brittany, I feel sure Sam is around somewhere. Now, don't you worry. You just keep trying his apartment. Good-bye, dear."

Brittany stared at the phone. Her father didn't sound like himself. And he didn't usually end conversations with her so abruptly. What was going on? But she couldn't worry about her father, not just now. She paced the living room, dialed Sam's number one more time, then stopped midstream. The key! Was it still here? She raced over to the hall secretary and there it was, the apartment key he had left with her. Just in case she ever needed him, he'd said. *Needed him?* She'd never known the human animal was capable of such need. It stopped her heart, spun her head, and was driving her crazy.

She stared first at the key, then looked down at Dunkin with a gleam in her eye. "Dunkin, prepare yourself. We're moving!"

Before she could think about it twice, she pulled an overnight case from the closet and threw in a toothbrush, a box of dog food, and a few other necessities, then slipped into her jacket and surveyed her home. Everything would be fine for a while. A smile slipped across her face. She'd be there for him whenever he came back. She'd be there to love him, no matter what.

It wasn't until she and Dunkin hurried out the front door that she noticed the weather. It was snowing, a soft light sprinkling that glittered against the bright sunlight. It was beautiful.

She lifted her head, her mouth open, and welcomed the wet flakes that landed on her cheeks and her tongue. "It's an omen, Dunkin. A good-luck omen."

They walked down the stairs carefully, Dunkin slipping near the end and skidding down the two last steps on his bottom. "Careful, boy," she said, laughing and rubbing his head. "We need to be in good shape for Sam."

The van was waiting, the key was clutched tightly in

her hand, and Brittany felt that finally, at last, all was almost right in the world.

The snow was falling more heavily as she pulled out onto the main street that would take her to the south side of town—and to Sam. She smiled as she maneuvered the van around parked cars, covered with a light frosting of snow. She loved it like this, the quiet, the untouched beauty, the feeling of wonder at the clean snow.

But mostly she loved Sam.

Her eyes were drawn for a moment to a small dog sitting on the sidewalk in the distance. He was infatuated with the snow, trying to catch the flakes in his paw. She smiled at his antics, remembering Dunkin when he was a puppy and how he'd bark furiously at snow. As she drew closer she noticed a little boy of eight or so come out of the house on the opposite side of the street, look around, and just as she came within hearing distance, call out to the dog.

The animal jerked its head around and in a split-second, flew out into the street toward the boy.

Brittany slammed on the brakes and leaned heavily on the wheel, pulling it to the right.

But the slippery surface of the new snow made her brakes useless, and as the dog scampered to safety, the van hopped the curb.

The last thing Brittany heard was the horrible crunch of metal as it folded around the fat trunk of an oak tree.

Thirteen

Sam's voice. She'd found him at last! He'd been . . . Where had he been?

Brittany slowly lifted her eyelids, then lowered them again, her hand moving automatically toward a painful spot on her head. As her fingers slid over the mound, she winced. What was happening?

There it was again, Sam's wonderful, deep voice. And he was saying her name now. Brittany Winters. She lifted her head and looked around, then sank back onto the hard surface and groaned.

An accident. The dog . . . the snow . . . and that huge tree that had leaped out in front of her. She tucked her chin down and surveyed her body groggily. It looked all right. She wiggled slightly. Owwww. Her eyes darted to her ankle and she spotted a thick Ace bandage wrapped around it. And her shoe sat next to it on the sheet.

Dunkin!

"Sam!"

The white curtains flew back and Sam was there, leaning over her, holding her and murmuring her name. "You sure know how to scare a guy."

"Dunkin. Oh, Sam, Dunkin was with me. . . ."

"Shh, darlin'." He kissed her forehead lightly. "He's fine. He came out of this better than you did. He's a terrific protector, Brittany. Wouldn't let the paramedics *touch* you until they showed IDs."

She breathed deeply and her eyelids closed halfway. "I'm so relieved he's okay."

"And I'm so relieved you're okay. If you only knew how worried I've been."

She looked up at him. Everything was so fuzzy, so foggy. She wished she could think more clearly. "Sam, how did you know . . . how did you know I was here?"

"Because, little lady, the *only* identification on you—you seemed to have left your purse at home—was a key to my apartment! I had tagged it with my address when I gave it to you." He wedged himself onto the examining table beside her and held both of her hands in his. His voice was husky and strain coated his words. "Brittany, where were you going?"

Her lips curled in a small smile. "I . . . was going to move in with you. Dunkin and I . . . we were going to risk it." She shook her head slowly. "No, excuse me. We *are* going to risk it." A tear meandered down her cheek. "Sam, I love you. And I want to be with you. Somehow we'll work all this out."

He slipped his hands beneath her head and drew her up to kiss her. "Oh, we will, will we?" He found it difficult to talk, difficult to tell her what was in his heart, what he had planned through two sleepless nights. For now, holding her in his arms was enough.

"Sam, I'm not thinking too clearly." This was probably all a dream, she thought. A dream with Sam loving her like that with his eyes. Those wonderful eyes . . .

"It's the medicine, Brittany. They gave you some pain killers for your ankle and for a couple of stitches they took in your leg."

Her brows drew together in concern.

"Don't worry, it's nothing serious. Actually, I think it's kind of sexy."

"Sam . . ."

The rustling of the crisp curtain and entrance of a white-coated gentleman stopped her sleepy words. "Well, I see you're awake, Ms. Winters. I'm Dr. Stanwick."

She smiled faintly.

"You came in with quite a bump on your head, but it's nothing to worry about. It was enough to knock you out briefly, but there's no sign of a concussion. We've told Mr. Lawrence here what to look for."

Sam grinned. "They've put me completely in charge of you."

The doctor continued in an efficient, clipped voice. "The pain medicine is what's making you groggy and what made you fall asleep. The dose was quite strong. You'll sleep well when you leave here. And that's going to be my only prescription. Sleep." He smiled at Sam and shook his hand. "Nice meeting you. Take good care of her, and you can leave any time now."

He started to walk out, then half-turned. "Oh, you can pick up the dog at the nurses' desk. I believe he's having a bowl of cereal. It was all they could find."

She laughed wearily as he let the curtain fall back in place, then focused all her feeble attention on Sam, who was scooping her up in his arms and holding her tight against his chest. She felt weak and strong, heavy and weightless all at once. "Oh, Sam, it wasn't supposed to be like this, you know. I had it all planned. . . ." Her voice drifted off and she struggled to keep her eyes open.

"No, it wasn't supposed to be like this. But as long as I have you now. Oh, Brittany . . . You're my life."

A small smile played on her lips as her eyelids fell heavily.

The snow had stopped and again had turned the world into a wonderland.

Sam smiled happily through the windshield and into

the dark night. Brittany was curled up next to him, her body wrapped in a warm blanket and her head resting against his shoulder. In the backseat Dunkin snored comfortably.

The few times Brittany had opened her eyes the past couple of hours, she had only murmured sleepily, then dropped off again, never asking where she was or why.

Evergreen was blinking its lights off in sleep when Sam passed through, and the narrow road to the cabin was lit by the huge moon hanging low in the sky.

Beside him, Brittany stirred.

"We're here, darlin'." He pulled the car to a stop beside the porch and turned off the engine.

Brittany opened her eyes and looked out into the black night. Her vision adjusted and she saw the moonlit snow and the cabin, lit like a beacon with light that filtered out through the curtains.

"Sam . . ."

"Come on." He opened the door and was around to her side before her sleepy mind had completely awakened.

In one smooth movement he slid his hands beneath her and lifted her gently from the car.

"I think there's something I should tell you," she murmured against his chest.

"Wait." After Dunkin jumped out, Sam shoved the door shut with his knee and walked slowly up the steps, carrying Brittany into the house. "Are you awake enough to know I just carried you across the threshold?"

"Yes," she whispered hoarsely. "But, Sam, it's somebody else's threshold. The cabin has been sold."

Sam was silent as he walked over to the couch and lowered her onto the cushions. Fumbling in his pocket, he pulled out a small envelope and laid it in her lap.

Brittany stared at it for a moment, then looked up at Sam. His lean figure was outlined in golden firelight. "Sam, what's going on here?"

"Wait, I've got my order of events all mixed up." When he slipped down on the woolly rug, she spotted the ice bucket behind him and the foil-wrapped top sticking out of it. The room was rosy and warm from the carefully banked fire, and the soft lights lit shadowy corners. And then her heart began to beat crazily as she looked into Sam's brown eyes.

"Brittany." He lifted both her hands to his lips as he knelt beside her, drawing his head close. "Will you marry me?"

Her heart stopped. "Oh, Sam—" She didn't want the tears to come, she'd shed enough for a lifetime, but when they did, he gently kissed them away.

"Is that a yes?"

"Oh, Sam, I love you so much. You know that, but are you sure? There are so many things we need to say."

He nodded against her cheek. "But not until I get my answer."

She framed his head between her hands and brought his mouth to hers, her pulse quickening. Words seemed inconsequential set against the incredible feeling that engulfed her, but she pulled back slightly and whispered against his lips, "Yes, my darling. Whenever you'd like. Now, tomorrow, next year . . . As long as I have you."

His arms were around her, holding her with tender passion. "It will be good, Brittany, I promise you."

She nodded and gazed at him through eyes grown misty. "And this?" She slipped her hand down and felt the stiff edge of the envelope.

"A wedding present." He took it from her and looked at it. "Chosen with great care and love."

She tilted her head back to one side. "Mighty sure of yourself, were you?"

He smiled. "Yes. And I knew if *I* wasn't enough, this would do it." He flapped the envelope against her hand. "This is no fly-by-night proposal you've got yourself here, Brittany Ellsbeth."

"Hmm. So the way to a woman's heart is . . ." She fluttered her eyelashes at him. "The envelope please?" Despite her joking, her hands were shaking as she eased a sheet of paper out of the envelope. Her eyes moved over it once, then again, then it slipped from her fingers and fluttered silently to the floor. "Oh, Sam."

"Am I going to spend the whole night kissing away a faceful of tears?" He leaned forward to rub his cheek along her damp face. "It seems a shame when there are so many other lovely parts of you to kiss."

"*You* . . . you bought the cabin . . ."

"My first permanent address since I was nineteen," he said proudly. "The way I figure it, we can use it on weekends and vacations—or even more often if we want. There's room here for the first four children, and then we can build an addition off the east wing if necessary. Did I ever tell you my mother was a twin?"

Brittany could only shake her head.

"Well, there'll be plenty of time for that. And eventually we can move our rocking chairs up here and retire."

"Sam, slow down." She covered his lips with her fingers. "I need to know . . . about your thinking, how you came to all this."

He eased himself up onto the couch next to her, and folded her into his arms. "It was the game, Brittany, the game that finally made me see things clearly. Every now and then in life you meet a kindred spirit, and as I poured myself into that game, I realized mine was your father.

"We're so much alike in what we want from life, the things we love, the needs we have. And until you, I'd categorized marriage as a definite roadblock to all those things.

"But your father had it all and more. We talked for a long long time, he and I."

"Saturday morning?"

"Yes, before I came up here to meet Ida and straighten the place up. Can't bring your intended to a dusty hideaway, you know." His fingers spread in slow motion through her hair, and he brushed it back and kissed the tip of her ear.

"But we talked at the party too. I knew the instant I saw you that night that no matter what, you couldn't walk out of my life. Your dad was a sounding board. I wanted to be sure I'd be good for you, too, even though I knew my life would be pretty worthless without you.

"He helped me see a lot of things clearly. The book I said I'd write, for example."

"In France . . ." Her voice was a whisper.

He nodded. "It's simple. A honeymoon trip to gather facts. And you'll meet my godchildren. Who knows?" He pressed a kiss into her hair. "Maybe it'll give us some ideas. . . . And then we'll come back and I'll write the book here, with the proper inspiration, of course." His words were whispered against her cheek. "And whatever happens after that, we'll work out together."

"Do you know what I think?" she said, unable to hear any more without crying again. Her mouth searched seductively for his and her fingers played with the buttons on his shirt.

Sam could only second-guess. "You want my body."

She undid the last button and slipped her hands inside to touch his warm skin. "And soul . . ."

"I'm in a very generous mood, my love. Is there anything else?" His hand slid beneath her sweater and he watched her eyes turn glassy when his fingers covered her breast.

The tears came anyway, rolling down her cheeks as she pressed her body against his with hungry desire. "You've given me everything, Sam," she whispered. "Your love, this place . . ."

His lips were parted and moist against her face, and he felt the urgency of his love stirring between his loins. "And it's all permanent, Brittany," he promised her huskily. "Without a doubt."

"And it feels right?" She nipped at his lower lip and felt his shiver all through her. "No second thoughts?"

"Oh, lots of second thoughts . . ." His hand was lacing her body with desire. "And third thoughts . . ." Heat trailed down her as his fingers journeyed lower.

"But those thoughts I'll show you, my Brittany . . ." And with gentle loving he slid their bodies down on the couch as the show began.

THE EDITOR'S CORNER

In celebration of our first anniversary we printed the following in our Editor's Corner—"It seems only a breathless moment ago that we launched LOVESWEPT into the crowded sea of romance publishing." Many things have happened in the years since we published the first LOVESWEPTs. The market has seen the birth of new romance lines and, sad to say, the demise of romance lines. Through it all we have remained true to the statement we made in our first anniversary issue—"Each time we've reached the goal of providing a truly fresh, creative love story, we find our goal expands, and we have a new standard of freshness and creativity to strive for." We try. Sometimes we don't hit on the mark. Sometimes we astonish even ourselves by hitting it square in the center. But thanks to the support of each of you, all the LOVESWEPT authors are growing and learning, while doing what we most like and want to do. We have even more of a challenge in presenting not just four, but six terrific romances each month.

It is such a pleasure to have a Helen Mittermeyer love story to kick off our expanded list next month. In **KISMET,** LOVESWEPT #210, Helen gives you another of her tempestuous romances with a heroine and hero who match each other in passion and emotional intensity. Tru Hubbard meets Thane Stone at one of the most difficult times in her life—certainly not the time to fall head-over-heels in love. Yet she does, and it looks as if she's rushing headlong into another emotionally disastrous situation, not just for herself, but for Thane, too. And so she runs as far and as fast as she can. But she's failed to realize her man is ready to walk through fire for her. A very exciting love story!

If there's a city more romantic than Paris, someone has failed to let me know. I think you'll love the setting almost as much as the heroine and hero in Kathleen Downes's LOVESWEPT #211, **EVENINGS IN PARIS.** From the moment Bart Callister spies a lovely mystery woman on the deck of the Eiffel Tower until he has pursued and caught lovely Arri Smith there's breathless, mysterious love and romance to charm you. But Arri's afraid. She knows she's no siren! You'll relish the ways that Bart handles her when she thinks *all* her secrets have been revealed. A true delight!

It is a great pleasure for me to introduce you to our new author Margie McDonnell and her poignant romance **BANISH THE DRAGONS,** LOVESWEPT #212. I had the pleasure of working with Margie before I came to Bantam, so I know she writes truly from knowledge of the heart and of courage, traits

(continued)

that she shows in her own life. Here she brings you a captivating couple, David and Angela, who know the worst that life has to offer and whose bravery and optimism and head-over-heels love will make you sing for joy, when you're not cheering them—and the children they deal with in a very special summer camp. A truly heartwarming, memorable debut.

Sit back, relax, and prepare to chuckle with glee and thrill to romance as you read Joan Elliott Pickart's **LEPRECHAUN,** LOVESWEPT #213. Imagine Blake Pemberton's shock when, home sick with the flu, a woman appears at his bedside who is so sprightly and lovely she seems truly to be one of the "little people" of Irish legend. And imagine Nichelle Clay's shock when she shows up to clean an apartment and confronts a sinfully gorgeous hunk wrapped in one thin sheet! A charming romp, first to last.

Welcome back Olivia and Ken Harper with **A KNIGHT TO REMEMBER,** LOVESWEPT #214. Tegan Knight sizzles with surprises for hero Jason Sloane, who is sure the T in her first name stands for Trouble. She'd do just about anything to thwart his business plans, but she hadn't counted on his plans for her! And those she cannot thwart—but what red-blooded woman would even want to? Two devilishly determined charmers make for one great romance.

LOVING JENNY, LOVESWEPT #215, showcases the creativity and talent of Billie Green. There are very few authors who could pull off what Billie does in this incredible story. Her heroine, Jenny Valiant, crashes her ex-husband's wedding reception to inform him their quickie divorce was as valid as a three dollar bill. Then she whisks him away (along with his bride) to sunny Mexico for another, but this time valid divorce, and sweeps them all into one of the most tender, touching, humorous romances of all time. A fabulous love story.

Enjoy!

Carolyn Nichols

Carolyn Nichols
Editor

LOVESWEPT
Bantam Books, Inc.
666 Fifth Avenue
New York, NY 10103